ON THE WAY TO GRETNA GREEN

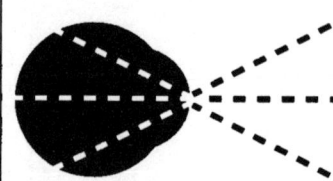

This Large Print Book carries the Seal of Approval of N.A.V.H.

ON THE WAY TO GRETNA GREEN

Marian Devon

G.K. Hall & Co. • Thorndike, Maine

Copyright © 1998 by Marian Pope Rettke

All rights reserved.

Published in 1998 by arrangement with Ballantine Books, a division of Random House, Inc.

G.K. Hall Large Print Paperback Series.

The text of this Large Print edition is unabridged. Other aspects of the book may vary from the original edition.

Set in 16 pt. Plantin by Juanita Macdonald.

Printed in the United States on permanent paper.

Library of Congress Cataloging in Publication Data

Devon, Marian.
   On the way to Gretna Green / Marian Devon.
      p.   cm.
   ISBN 0-7838-0381-8 (lg. print : sc : alk. paper)
   1. Large type books.   I. Title.
[PS3554.E9282705   1998]
813'.54—dc21   98-41392

ON THE WAY TO GRETNA GREEN

Chapter One

"Go back to sleep, blast you!"

Miss Claudia Wentworth glared at the three indifferent donkeys.

Despite her whip and the use of language more suited to a groom than a lady of quality, they had pulled her phaeton at an infuriating crawl for the full five miles that separated her brother's house from Hunter's Hall. Now she dropped the reins, grabbed up her skirts immodestly, leapt out of the carriage, and raced toward a looming edifice that to her jaundiced eyes seemed more fit for a prison than a country house. "Thank God for moonlight," she thought as she shivered in the late winter chill. But then, of course there would be moonlight. Even those two ninnyhammers would have made sure of that.

Skirts in hand, she took the flight of crumbling steps leading to the portico at an imperiled run. She plied the iron knocker with enough clamor to wake the dead, then welcomed the chance to catch her breath while waiting for an answer. She soon found herself waiting and waiting. Her breath was not only quite restored but likely to convert to dragon fire as she was forced to clang away once more. With identical results.

No one home? She knew better. Gone to bed? Well, hardly. The place was ablaze with light.

Claudia gave the heavy ornate handle a furious twist, and to her amazement the massive door creaked open.

She stepped into a hall that at another time might have overawed her by its size, its marble floor, its marble statuary, but she was impervious to grandeur at the moment. Her eyes were riveted instead upon a figure shuffling toward her with all the vigor of her sleepy donkeys. "He's ancient" was her first thought as she took in the footman's shuffling gait. "He's foxed" was her next assessment as he drew nearer. He was holding a candle aloft in a shaky hand, an unnecessary as well as a hazardous accessory in the well-lit hall. Bright blue livery did not obscure a dirty nightshirt, and his powdered wig sat sideways atop his head.

Claudia's face reflected her disgust.

The footman's face was equally disapproving. No lady would call unaccompanied on a bachelor establishment at any time, let alone at such an ungodly hour. As for a light-skirt — well, this one was a disgrace to the sisterhood. Imagine showing herself to a Bond Street beau, wearing a drab-colored hooded cloak more fit to blanket a horse than turn a gentleman's head. Unfortunately, the servant's attempt at starchiness was overset by his slurred diction. "His lordship is not at home," he enunciated thickly. A sudden burst of raucous laughter made a mockery of his words.

"The devil he isn't!"

Claudia pushed past the protesting footman and followed the noise. It led her through the hall into an enormous, elegantly appointed, quite empty saloon, where she paused a moment to listen, then traced the sounds to an antechamber on her right. There she was forced once more to wait on the threshold as her eyes teared in defense against the clouds of smoke and lingering fumes caused by cigars both past and present. She blinked to clear them, then focused upon a baize-covered card table, the center of the storm. Four men were grouped around it, appearing at first glance even more inebriated than the footman. "Blast!" She squared her shoulders, took a deep breath — instantly regretted — then strode purposefully into the room and up to the table.

"I need to speak to Lord Thornton. Urgently."

Three jaws dropped. Three pairs of bloodshot eyes widened. The fourth, blue and no less bloodshot, impaled her.

"Do I know you?"

The voice was imperious and surprisingly unslurred considering the two-day growth of beard, the rumpled ash-strewn cambric shirt, the dark hair whose overgrown Brutus cut was in shocking disarray.

"If you do, pray introduce me," one leering cardplayer guffawed, and Claudia, no stranger to imperiousness herself, gave the baby-faced wit a set-down stare. The other two inebriates found this exchange hilarious. "No fair keeping this beauty to yourself," one chortled, assessing the intruder through an upside-down quizzing glass. The other cardplayer looked admiringly at his host. "My God, Thorn, how do you do it? You invite us down for a strictly bachelor party, and females still pursue you. By Jove, that Byron cove could take lessons."

"Lord Thornton!" Claudia had managed to ignore the banter, but it took some effort not to stamp her foot. "My business is most urgent, else I would not be here. I must speak to you in private."

Under better circumstances his lordship might have been considered almost handsome. His features were strong and regular, though not improved at the moment by an expression that conveyed annoyance mixed with disapproval. His eyes, usually his greatest claim to good looks, were narrowed as he scowled up at her.

"Miss Whoever You Are, this hand is *my* business, and it is also urgent. These so-called gentlemen have abused my hospitality and fleeced my pockets. And now that I am about to get my own back, I am not going to be diverted by unknown, uninvited females. So if you will find a seat, preferably back in the hall, I will be with you when our game is finished."

Claudia repressed a fishwifely urge to scream abuse. Instead she counted ten. Then walked calmly around the table to peer over his lordship's shoulder. "Well, unless you are a complete flat, it should not take too long, since you appear to be holding all the diamonds. No, I do beg pardon. The trey is missing."

"Damnation!"

His lordship threw his hand down in disgust while his opponents whooped and applauded.

"Well, you win, it seems. Excuse me, gentlemen." He shoved his chair back from the table. "Come on," he scowled at Claudia. "And I tell you now your visit had best be to some purpose, or else I may forget I am a gentleman and have you thrown out."

He led her, pointedly, back through the hall and into an antechamber nearest the entrance, where he stood with his back to the fireplace and his arms crossed. He did not, she noted, ask her to be seated. "Now, what the devil is this all about? And who the deuce are you?"

"I am Miss Wentworth of Fairwood, and this is about the elopement of your brother and my niece."

"The devil you say!"

"I do say, and I do not wish to waste any more time. For they are well on their way to Gretna Green by now. I can fill in details as we go. What I need from you is help in tracking them down and putting a stop to this insanity."

"My help?" His eyebrows rose. "Wouldn't that be more in Sir Edwin's province? I do have the name right?" She nodded. "I can't see myself in hot pursuit of a pair of infatuated halflings. To use a cliché, I am not my brother's keeper, Miss Wentworth."

"You had better be. For I cannot speak for my

brother's action when he discovers that the Honorable Rupert Hunt has run off with his only child."

Lord Thornton came close to sneering. "I do not wish to be offensive, but as I recall, your brother is not what one would term a bruiser. Even a no-goer like Rupert should be able to hold his own in such a matchup. Besides, again not wishing to be offensive, I should think that after the first shock wears off, Sir Edwin will be delighted. I doubt he could aspire quite so high."

Claudia all but ground her teeth. "Your lordship is wasting time. You may consider your brother above my niece's touch, but I can assure you, were he heir to the throne and still a Hunt, Sir Edwin would be enraged."

"My God." A sudden grin split his lordship's face. "You surely aren't pulling a Montague and Capulet, are you? Why, that squabble between our families dates back to my grandfather's day or before, I collect. Damned if I even know what it was about."

"Your grasp of family history is hardly the point." Claudia tightened the rein on her temper. "Lord Thornton, my niece is not yet sixteen years old. I doubt that your brother is much older. This elopement is folly and must be stopped. Unfortunately — or fortunately — my brother is away on business. He has taken our carriage. Now, if you will not help me pursue the runaways, at least furnish me with the means to do so on my own."

"Give you carte blanche with my cattle? You're mad!"

"Then, I can only regret wasting my time. Get back to your card game, Lord Thornton." She wheeled to leave.

"Just a moment. You can fly down from the boughs. I mean to help you. Your point about the ages of the imbeciles is well-taken. Besides, my mother won't be best pleased with the match. No off—"

"If you say 'no offense' once more, Lord Thornton, I shall scream this hideous house down."

"Then, I will propose another reason for my mother's opposition to the match. She will, no doubt" — he suddenly shook with laughter — "recall the bad blood between our families."

Claudia did not try to hide her disgust. "On top of everything else, you must be foxed."

"Foxed? Indeed not. Faintly disguised, perhaps, but certainly not foxed. I never overindulge at cards. I can assure you that I am sufficiently sober to have played my winning hand to perfection if you had not —"

"Oh, for God's sake, quit your prosing and let us go. They could be halfway to Gretna Green by now, and all you can think of is your curst cards!"

"Waspish ain't you? Do you think we might spare the time for me to bid my guests goodbye?"

She looked alarmed. "Don't you dare tell them where we are going! If word of this elopement gets out, my niece's reputation will be torn to shreds."

"You mean she has one? No" — he held up a restraining hand — "don't fly up into the boughs again. The remark was most uncalled for." He started toward the door. "I will only be a moment. And no, I won't tell them where I'm going. But I should warn you" — he grinned — "what they'll be thinking will be much worse."

"I am aware of that. But if you do not blurt out my name, it shouldn't matter. I am not acquainted with any of your friends, nor am I like to be." Her nose wrinkled.

Claudia quickly positioned herself by the front door to wait with her eyes glued upon a longcase clock placed in an alcove. Her resolve to go drag his lordship by the collar if he dawdled proved unnecessary. He returned in less than the five minutes she had allotted, now wearing a curly-brimmed beaver and a long-tailed coat of dark blue superfine, and holding a cravat in his hand. He glanced around for the absent footman, swore under his breath, then strode for a bellpull and gave it several yanks.

"For heaven's sake, can't you open a door for yourself? If not, allow me. I managed it before."

"Don't be such a sapskull!" The yanks on the pull continued. This time the footman arrived on the run. He appeared a bit more sober and a lot more disheveled. "Go to the stables and have my barouche sent around. And be damned quick about it."

As the footman sped back through the hall, his lordship opened the front door with a flourish, as though to prove he could. "After you, Miss Wentworth."

She stumbled a bit going down the crumbling steps, and he took her arm. She quickly pulled away. This was no time to play the helpless female. He shrugged and wound the cravat around his collar without the benefit of a looking glass or valet. The results set her teeth on edge.

"My God! What is that?"

His lordship stood transfixed, staring at her equipage.

"*That* is a phaeton."

Her tone should have closed the subject. It did not.

"You must be funning. It's like no phaeton I ever saw. And I presume those are bits of blood?"

The three donkeys, perhaps sensing that they were under scrutiny, opened sleepy eyes and shook their harnesses.

"There is no need to be insulting. Did I not make it plain that if I had the proper equipage, I would have no need of you?"

"Oh, yes, indeed. Quite plain. In fact —"

He was interrupted by the sound of a carriage sweeping up the drive. A coachman pulled it skillfully to a halt behind the donkeys. If he was astonished at this conveyance, or the lateness of the hour, or the young lady preparing to clamber into his carriage before it came properly to a halt, he was too well schooled to show it. He jumped down, intending to help the lady into the passenger's seat. His expression slipped a bit, however, as his master boosted her up into the box.

"Never mind, Jem. I intend to drive. Will you take that — thing — to the stables? And if we are not back, deliver it to Fairwood tomorrow."

Lord Thornton vaulted into the driver's seat.

"I assume you do know the way to Gretna Green?" Claudia queried.

"Not from firsthand experience, if that is what you mean. Hasty marriage — or any other kind, come to that — has no appeal for me." He cracked his whip and sprang his horses. She hung on for dear life as he circled on two wheels, then sped off down the graveled driveway. "All right?" He grinned down at her evilly.

"Perfectly, I assure you. But you, sir, are foxed."

"Think so?" He guided the carriage at increased speed through the narrow arch that formed the entrance to his estate. She could not quite prevent a gasp, and he laughed aloud. "You did say you were in a hurry, did you not?"

"Yes, I did." She spoke through gritted teeth. "But I would like to catch the runaways, not wind up with a broken neck in some ditch."

They were out on the highway now, and he began to slow his cattle.

"Lord Thornton! It is quite obvious to me that, drunk or sober, you are an accomplished whip. But your technique is mystifying. Not to say idiotic. Why, now that it is finally safe to proceed at your rackety speed, have you decided to inch along? Why, my donkeys could — My God, are we stopping?"

"Pausing is more like it. Here, move over." He was climbing across her. And as he did so, he thrust the reins into her hands. "Have you ever driven anything besides those asses? No matter. The question's academic. It's bright moonlight, the road is deserted, and my cattle are intelligent enough to drive themselves."

He settled beside her, then gave an earsplitting whistle that made both her and the horses jump. She clutched the reins in a death grip just in time to prevent their being jerked from her hands by the bolting cattle.

"Good work," he grinned, then tilted the beaver over his eyes and slouched down into his seat.

"You *are* foxed."

She made her point again, if truth be told, less as a lecture than a distraction. For she was struggling not to panic at being left in charge of a pair of thoroughbreds, the likes of which had never seen the inside of a Fairwood stable.

"My dear Miss Wentworth, you are becoming boring. What are you? Some rabid teetotaler? What I have drunk has nothing to say to the situation. I have not slept for some fifty or so hours. And there seems no time like the present. Good night, Miss Wentworth."

He was soon breathing deeply. Deep breathing progressed to snoring. Miss Wentworth found the sound decidedly annoying, but not nearly so annoying, she soon discovered, as when his lordship's head came to rest upon her shoulder.

Chapter Two

The bright moonlight, the high-stepping matched grays, the well-sprung carriage, not to mention the head upon her shoulder, were enough to distract her from her fury and anxiety about Evelina. She had removed his hat when it seemed in danger of blowing off. Thornton's snoring had finally died down to a gentle rhythm. He still smelled of stale cigars — a mercy perhaps, since he had doubtlessly not bathed any more recently than he had shaved.

She rounded a curve rather skillfully, she thought, but the change of direction roused her companion. He stretched his neck to look up at her through half-closed eyes and murmured "Sophy?"

"Sophy is not with us, my lord."

"What the devil?" He jerked upright, clutched his head, and groaned. "Oh, now I remember." There seemed little joy in the recollection. "At least we're still all in one piece, I see. Congratulations. I'll relieve you now."

"No need." She pointed with her whip up ahead where lamplight competed feebly with the moon. "That must be a posting house."

"Then, I will definitely drive."

He began to climb over her while she protested. "I am quite capable of turning into an inn yard — *oof!*" The barouche had hit a pothole that landed him in her lap. "Clumsy!" she fumed when she'd recovered sufficient breath.

"Who's clumsy? You were supposed to slide out from under me." Still atop her, he grabbed the reins and gave them a flip that urged on the horses.

"Move, Lord Thornton, blast it!"

"For a puritanical Wentworth, you have a nasty mouth."

"You're squashing the breath out of me!"

"Not sufficiently, it seems."

He guided the grays through the narrow archway. The inn yard was deserted at that hour except for a young ostler roused from a stolen nap. The lad rubbed his eyes sleepily, then rubbed them again to make certain he'd just seen what he thought he'd seen. Sure enough, the added clarity made it certain — a toff was driving a bang-up rig while seated on a lady's lap. There was no accounting for the gentry.

The gentleman flung him the reins, then jumped from the box to help the lady down. "We need a change of horses, the best you have. And handle that pair with kid gloves, or I'll have your hide when I come back for 'em." He was digging in his pocket as he spoke, and gave the lad a coin far more influential than his threats. Claudia was relieved to see the fatness of his purse. She grudgingly admitted to herself that he'd shown more forethought than she had.

"By the by," he asked the youngster, who was in the act of uncoupling the grays, "did a young lady and gentleman, unaccompanied, happen to pass through here?"

The ostler gave him a crafty look. "Lor', sir, young couples pass through 'ere in a steady stream, you might say, since The Crown 'ere is on the way to Gretna Green. They all begin to look alike, if you'll pardon me saying so. Course me memory could be jogged."

"And you could feel the sole of my boot on your backside before you get any more brass from me. Now, answer my question. The young gentleman would be about seventeen, fair-haired, a little shorter than me, five-ten or so."

The stable boy faked concentration. "Oh, now I recollects. With a real beauty, was he, with darkish 'air and eyes?"

Thornton looked a question at Claudia, who nodded.

"Looks nothing like you, then, does she?"

"No" was the starchy reply.

"No need to take offense," he said, grinning. "I was referring to your fair hair and blue? gray? eyes, not to the beauty thing."

He turned back to the ostler. "That's the pair. How long ago did you see them?"

The lad scratched his head. "Above two hours, I'd say."

"Well, hurry with the horses."

"Do you want a cup of tea or anything?" he asked his companion.

"No, let's not waste time. We need to catch them."

"Don't need to hurry, then," the boy offered as he prepared to lead his lordship's horses to the stables. "They're spending the night 'ere."

"Oh, dear God!" Claudia breathed.

"Are you sure of that?" Lord Thornton looked thunderous.

"Of course I'm sure. Broke a trace, didn't 'e, when he pulled in 'ere? Wonder was it made it this far, for a bigger piece of junk I never did see. The lady wasn't 'alf pleased," he called after them as they ran toward the inn. "In a fair state she was!"

The traveler's room in The Crown was small and dingy, equipped with a clock and a mirror and a bar. At the latter a young man wearing a three-caped greatcoat was dozing with his head in his hands and an untouched mug of ale in front of him. A young lady in a modish cherry pelisse with matching bonnet sat huddled by the gasping embers of the fireplace on the opposite side of the room. She was sniveling into a lace handkerchief. From its soggy state, the process must have been going on for some little time.

"Evelina!" Claudia hurried toward her.

Lord Thornton moved more sedately to the bar, where he drank deeply from his brother's mug before shaking him by the shoulder. "Wake up, Rupert. It's doomsday!"

Miss Evelina Wentworth jumped to her feet and threw her arms about her aunt. "Claudia, you've come! You are actually here! Thank God!"

Claudia had been far too occupied with the problems of pursuit to try and imagine what her reception might be when her goal was accomplished. But in her wildest imagination, she would not have foreseen this.

"Thank God you are here!" Evelina repeated before her increased sobs made further communication impossible.

Lord Thornton looked down at his sleep-bemused brother and glowered. "Don't tell me you actually kidnapped that female."

The accusation snapped Rupert awake. "Don't be a sapskull. Of course I didn't. Nothing of the kind."

"Then, why the waterfall?"

"You'll have to ask her that." His voice was laced with bitterness. He appeared to have aged since his brother had last seen him. His brown eyes had lost their innocent-puppy look, and his fair hair seemed a precursor of gray. "She's done nothing but wail for the past two hours."

It was unnecessary for Thornton to pose any more questions. The younger Miss Wentworth was in the process of pouring her heart out to her aunt, impeded though she was by sobs and the fact that her face was buried in Claudia's shoulder.

"It has all b-been dreadful. Simply dreadful. I thought running away would be r-romantic, but it wasn't like that at all. It was d-dreadful."

"There, there." Claudia patted the girl's back ineffectively while she glared at Lord Thornton, who had the insensitivity to grin. "It is all right now. I can see you have learned your lesson."

"Oh, I've learned all right. I have learned that *he*" — she gestured dramatically toward the bar without looking up, which meant she missed the Honorable Rupert's incensed reaction to the loathing expressed by a simple pronoun — "has not the slightest idea of how an elopement should be properly conducted."

"That is a contradiction in terms, my dear." Her aunt felt compelled to insert a lecture here, tame stuff compared to the neck-wringing she had planned. "There is no such thing as a 'proper elopement.' Especially for someone of your tender years."

"Well, there is such a thing as doing a thing right once you've started it." Indignation was winning out over the floodgates. Evelina raised her head to glare in the bridegroom's direction. "First of all, you would not believe the shabby rig he drove. Why, my abigail would not elope in such a thing."

"Would you believe," the Honorable Rupert addressed his brother, but in carrying tones, "the widgeon thought I should actually call for her in your traveling coach. Of all the sapskulls. God knows what you would have said to that."

"Very little, actually. Murder springs to mind."

"And, as if that weren't bad enough," the younger Miss Wentworth continued, "when the pathetic thing fell to pieces, as any flat should have known it would, and we had to stop in this awful place, it seems he did not bother to bring sufficient funds to hire a private parlor, not even to mention a bed for me." She dissolved into tears again.

"Rather expensive this married life, is it?" Thornton grinned at his brother.

"Lord Thornton, your levity is entirely inappropriate. I suggest that you see to the change of horses, and we take these children home," Claudia said impatiently.

"We c-can't go home," Evelina wailed.

"Indeed we can. Immediately."

"No no." The tone was tragic. "We have to go on to Gretna Green."

"You can't be serious." Claudia refused to believe her ears. "To even think of this ill-conceived marriage after all you've just said?"

"But we must get married, don't you see."

This declaration was followed by a shocked silence.

"You can't be serious," Claudia finally repeated.

"She's right, you know." Rupert could not hide his despair.

"Good God!" Lord Thornton looked thunderstruck. "You mean that you actually — Good God, Rupert. I gave you credit for more sense. Not to mention principles!"

"Now, just a minute." Rupert straightened up to glare indignantly. "Surely you ain't thinking! That's a damn slander, that is."

"Well, what am I supposed to think?"

"That some nosey old harpy that Evelina knows came in here and saw us together, and now she" — he gestured brideward — "says we have to go through with the wedding, though I don't mind saying I'd rather be drawn and quartered."

"And just how do you think I feel?" The halflings exchanged glares while their elders counted ten.

"Isn't that a bit extreme?" Lord Thornton's eyebrows rose. "Legshackled for life to avoid a little gossip?"

"A little gossip. A *little* gossip!" Evelina cut off her renewed sobbing to give her almost brother a lethal glare. "That's all very well for you to say. Or Rupert, either, for that matter. He'll merely be a nine days' wonder while I shall be r-ruined for life. Now no one will have me!" she finished in a wail.

"Not if they've a brain in their heads," the bridegroom muttered.

"No more of that," his brother muttered back.

"Is it really that serious?" His lordship addressed the question to the elder Miss Wentworth.

"I am not sure. Who was it who saw you, Evelina?"

"That odious Mrs. Railton, that's who. And sh-she's the biggest gossipmonger in the county."

Claudia answered Lord Thornton over her niece's shoulder. "I fear it is quite serious. But you are right. Marriage is not the answer. What's done is done, Evelina. You will simply have to live down the talk. This will all be forgot in time."

"It will not! People will chew on it for the rest of my life. 'There goes Miss Evelina Wentworth — have you heard?' No, I cannot endure it. I will have to marry — *him*." Again the pronoun was packed with loathing.

"Oh, come now. You cannot be seriously considering marriage with a young man you appear to despise. This is the height of folly."

"What choice do I have? No one else will have me now. And I do not wish to wind up an old maid ape leader like you."

Lord Thornton looked startled and stared harder at his companion of the evening. With an effort Claudia refrained from boxing her niece's ears.

"Perhaps we can save you from that fate worse than death," she said dryly, "without going through with this elopement. After all, I am here now to serve as chaperon. Perhaps we can convince Mrs. Railton that I have been with you all along."

"Why, yes. That's a capital plan," Thornton interposed sarcastically. "You and I here together. That should strike the gossipmongers silent. In spite of your niece's reference to your advanced years, I doubt your antiquity makes you immune to wagging tongues."

"Well then, just what do you suggest? On to Gretna Green?"

Rupert turned even paler. "Thorn!" he wailed.

"God, no. If these two imbeciles marry, chances are that they'd have progeny, a thought that makes me shudder for the future of the race."

"We would do no such thing!" Evelina raised her head and her voice. "I do not intend to ever speak to him again, let alone —" She stopped and blushed.

"And that is fine with me!" her sweetheart retorted.

"Children!" Claudia was beginning to feel like a put-upon governess. A governess with the beginnings of a megrim. "Pray stifle your bickering while we decide what is best to be done." She hated herself for it, but she looked imploringly at his lordship. "Do you have a suggestion?"

"I most certainly have."

Years of breeding were evident in the fifth viscount's tone. "First we will engage that private parlor your niece has been pining for and have some supper. Then I propose to arrange bedrooms for what is left of the night. Two bedrooms. As far as possible from one another. Perhaps in the morning we can all be a bit more rational.

"Tell me, is that curst postboy the only creature awake in this so-called inn?" The question was addressed to Rupert.

"As far as I know."

"Well, then."

His lordship strode across the room, opened

the outer door, and shouted. "You there! Ostler!"

"That should get the attention of the entire staff, not to mention the sleeping travelers," Claudia remarked to the unresponsive ceiling, as she braced herself for what would be a long night.

Chapter Three

The inn began to spring to life, at least as far as its staff was concerned. A frowsy maid, who had abandoned her post for a stolen snooze, emerged first to begin wiping the counter industriously with a weather eye cocked toward the stairway. She was just in time. The portly, balding landlord soon came rushing down it, buttoning a straining waistcoat as he came. He was joined by a yawning waiter.

Claudia could hear Lord Thornton issuing orders as he left to see to his cattle. She did not hesitate to countermand them when the obsequious host hurried to usher them toward a private parlor with the promise of a cold collation soon to follow. She could think of nothing worse than forcing the warring elopers to spend more time together. "My niece and I will go directly to our bedchamber," she informed the landlord. "Would you like something sent to our rooms, Evelina?"

"I am not hungry, thank you." The tone was martyred. "I doubt I shall ever be again."

"Fustian!" the Honorable Rupert snorted. "Then, why were you raising such a dust when I couldn't afford to wine and dine you?"

"That was hours ago," the other glared. "Before I had the slightest —"

"That will do!" Claudia snapped. She turned back to the host, who was struggling to keep his face impassive, though his eyes betrayed a lively interest in the unfolding drama. "I am sure the gentlemen need their supper. But if you could send up a pot of tea along with buttered toast, I would be most grateful. And, oh, yes, could you manage a poultice? I seem to have developed a frightful headache."

The two ladies were soon settled, but sleep was slow to come. Claudia had placed the alum-and-egg-white-soaked cloth upon her forehead, but its efficacy was suspect. Or perhaps it was her niece's unsuccessful attempts to smother her sobs, as she lay beside her on the feather bed, that made it impossible to sleep. All in all, she decided, Lord Thornton's snores were preferable. She was finally drifting off into the arms of Morpheus when an errant thought jerked her wide awake again. Just who the deuce is Sophy?

Then, when she actually did succumb, she was roused by an irritating tapping. She was forming the words to command her servants to delay hanging pictures in the hallway until morning, for heaven's sake, when she came to the realization that it was morning, that she was not at Fairwood, that Evelina was sound asleep beside her, and someone was tapping at their door. She groped for her dressing gown, then remembered she had lain down fully clothed.

"Well, you certainly look burnt to the socket."

Claudia was tempted to slam the door in

Thornton's grinning face. She berated herself silently for not taking the time to at least smooth her tousled hair before opening it.

He seemed to read her mind as his eyes traveled over her rumpled, drab-colored round dress. "You could, perhaps, thank God for your cloak and hood."

The worst of it was that his lordship's appearance had vastly improved. For one thing, he was now clean shaven. For another, where on earth had he found fresh linen?

"Rise and shine, Miss Wentworth!" he called over Claudia's shoulder. Evelina was sitting up in bed, staring their way uncomprehendingly. "We must leave immediately."

"Without tea?" Claudia's reaction was reflex.

"We can manage that a bit later." He lowered his voice. "I think you will agree once you've regained consciousness that saving reputations is our first order of business. And speaking of which, pray allow me to present my aunt."

Claudia had just become aware that a tall, distinguished lady was emerging from the next-door chamber. The sight of her gray bombazine carriage dress, of the latest fashion, sank Claudia's self-esteem even lower, a state she would have thought impossible.

"Lady Harville," Lord Thornton said formally, "allow me to present the two Miss Wentworths."

"You may dispense with ceremony, James." Lady Harville's brusqueness was softened by a warm smile and nod toward the younger women. "We should waste no time. The public coach will soon be leaving."

"True. Hurry up, ladies. Five minutes. No more. We'll wait right here." He gave Claudia a gentle shove back into her chamber and closed the door between them.

"Who does he think he is to order us about like —"

Claudia cut Evelina's protest short. "I don't think this is the time for that. The important thing is, Lord Thornton appears to have furnished us with a chaperon. Let us simply do what he has asked."

"Asked? Commanded, don't you mean?"

"I suppose so. But we are in no position to stand on points. Splash some water on your face and hold this thought: The sooner we make ourselves available, the sooner we'll be free of his imperious lordship."

"And his odious brother." Evelina, ignoring the washbasin, clapped her bonnet on her head and gave the strings a jerk.

"That's the spirit."

The Wentworths hurried from the room to join their titled escorts.

"Do we pass muster?" Claudia refused to be flustered by his lordship's appraising stare.

"You will have to, won't you?" He stepped back to allow them to follow Lady Harville, who was already hurrying down the corridor. "At least your niece has stopped sniveling," he remarked when Evelina had got out of earshot. "That is progress — Damnation!" He stopped in his tracks halfway down the stairs. "I hope we aren't too late."

A crowd was milling about impatiently near the inn's entrance awaiting the London stage. "Ah." He relaxed. "That must be the harpy guarding all those boxes." He gestured toward a Christmas pudding of a woman wearing a voluminous brown cloak and a green bonnet adorned with bobbing red berries. "Am I not right?"

"Oh, my heavens, yes."

Claudia fought to keep her face free from consternation as Evelina froze in her tracks and looked back at them like a cornered rabbit. "But how did you know?"

"Rupert just signaled." And for the first time Claudia noticed the bridegroom, concealed behind three military men bunched in conversation just a few feet away from the gossipmonger. "Besides, who could mistake the type? But try not to look quite so Friday-faced. The important thing is that we've caught her in time. I had hoped to acquaint you with your lines before you were thrust into performance, but never mind. All you need do is present her to your hostess — Lady Harville, in case you've forgot the name — then follow my aunt's lead. She will do the rest. Ah, we have been spotted. Places, everyone." He grinned at the two apprehensive ladies. "Curtain going up!"

Mrs. Railton had indeed spied the group coming down the staircase. Her raisin eyes, lost though they were in a surround of fat, still managed to widen in surprise. " 'Pon my soul! It is *both* the Miss Wentworths!" she announced to the world at large. The other passengers separated widely to allow her to pass through them. "I did see Miss Evelina down here last night, Miss Wentworth," she continued in her carrying voice as she managed to halt the descending party by the simple expedient of placing herself at the bottom of the stairs. "But I am amazed to see you here, as well."

"Indeed?" Claudia's eyebrows rose. "Now *I* am amazed. I should have thought that once you noticed my niece, my presence would have been anticipated."

"But pray allow me to make you acquainted with the rest of our party. Lady Harville, Lord Thornton, may I present Mrs. Railton, our vicar's wife? Lady Harville is his lordship's aunt, Mrs. Railton."

His lordship removed his beaver and executed a perfunctory bow.

Her ladyship smiled graciously. "The vicar's wife? Then, it is your husband's church I admired as we rode through the village. Norman, no doubt?"

"Oh, indeed. You are acquainted with Mansfield, your ladyship?" Mrs. Railton fairly quivered with curiosity.

"Alas, only slightly. My nephew here escorted

me from London, and we passed through your charming village in order to collect the two Miss Wentworths, who have graciously consented to spend some time with me at Harville Hall."

Under different circumstances Claudia would have been quite diverted by Mrs. Railton's eager fawning. But then, under different circumstances, she could not imagine Lady Harville divulging so much of her personal business to this gossipy toadeater.

"Now, if you will excuse us." Lord Thornton did not bother with an excess of civility. His tone made it obvious, to Claudia at least, that their mission was accomplished. "I believe our breakfast is waiting."

Miss Railton stepped aside and unblocked their passage. But she grasped Claudia's arm to detain her. "A quick word, Miss Wentworth," she whispered.

Claudia paused reluctantly as the others proceeded toward a private parlor.

"You know I never wish to pry — or tell tales out of school." Fortunately, Mrs. Railton did not require a reply to this blatant untruth, but plowed ahead. "However, I do feel a duty, both as vicar's wife and, I trust, as friend" — Fortunately again, no confirmation of the latter intimacy was required — "to inform you that I saw your niece — unattended — in the traveler's room, late at night, with a young gentleman."

"Evelina?" Claudia's ingenuousness implied that she had any number of nieces to choose from. "How very odd." She frowned in concentration, and then her expression cleared. "Oh, now I recall. Why, yes, of course. She was complaining of aches in her limbs from being cooped up in a carriage so long, and I suggested that she walk about a bit. It did not occur to me, I fear, to tell her to avoid the public room. It was remiss of me. I shall certainly speak to her of it."

"You should warn her about appearances, Miss Wentworth." Mrs. Railton's mouth was prim. "She was, you see, alone with the young man. Oh, I say! There he goes now."

The Honorable Rupert had lagged behind the rest, hoping to sneak into the parlor unobserved by the busybody. He was unsuccessful.

"Oh, that young man." Claudia breathed a stagy sigh. "Well, that is certainly a relief. I can see why my niece felt compelled to exchange civilities. He is his lordship's brother, you see, and one of our party."

"Humph!" Some of the wind had left Mrs. Railton's sails, but she was by no means becalmed. "Be that as it may, it would certainly have appeared odd to anyone who happened to see them. I do not mind admitting, Miss Wentworth, that at first I feared the two must be eloping."

"Did you indeed?" Claudia contrived to produce a laugh. "Evelina and the Honorable Rupert Hunt eloping? This is too droll for words. Why, they can scarcely abide one another — are always at daggers drawn. I must say, I am amazed that Evelina even bothered to do the polite."

"Well, as a matter of fact" — Mrs. Railton looked rather crestfallen — "they did seem to have little to say to one another when I observed them."

"I am not surprised. But now, if you will excuse me, I fear I am delaying our departure."

Claudia hurried away thankfully, feeling that disaster had indeed been averted.

Mrs. Railton gazed after her, a puzzled frown creasing her plump face.

Chapter Four

Sir Edwin Wentworth's traveling coach turned into the gates of his estate and followed a donkey-drawn conveyance up the drive. Leaning far out his window to see what was impeding their progress, he thought he recognized the phaeton. But the driver of the vehicle had him puzzled. If Claudia had taken it upon herself to hire another servant in his absence . . . well, she had taken a great deal too much upon herself was all that he could say. He shouted at the coachman to take him on to the stables in order to solve the mystery.

"I say, who exactly are you?" he asked as he descended the lowered steps and frowned down at a stunted lad of twelve whose impish features seemed incapable of arranging themselves into an expression of proper respect. The boy stood by the donkeys' heads, holding one of the bridles (more from habit than necessity, since these animals were no more likely to bolt than a trio of snails) while he looked impatiently around for someone to relieve him of his charges. He pushed back the jockey cap he wore — bright blue to match what was probably a short coat on the original owner but in his case reached the buttocks — and revealed a head of sandy hair as overgrown as his costume.

"Me name is Jocko, sir." The "sir" was slow in coming. The lad did not care for this toff's tone above half.

"That tells me very little." Sir Edwin, fatigued from a wasted journey and a long, jolting drive, possessed little patience. "Did my sister employ you?"

"Not to me knowledge. But then, I ain't acquainted with your sister, am I? She could 'ave 'ad an influence for all I know, sir."

"None of your impudence. Explain yourself. What are you doing with my rig?"

"Returning it."

"Returning it? From where? And mind you give me a straight answer."

"From Hunter's Hall."

"From Hunter's Hall!" Sir Edwin fairly reeled with shock. "But that is impossible! Why was my rig at Hunter's Hall?"

Lord Thornton's tiger was suddenly enjoying himself. He had suffered the indignity of prodding those worthless excuses for cattle all the way here, and lucky it was that no one he knew had seen him. He, Jocko Fox, who had often voiced his ambition of someday holding the ribbons and blowing the yard of tin on the stage to York, to be spotted driving donkeys! Why, he'd never live it down. But now it was worth the aggravation just to see this puffed-up swell test the limits of apoplexy.

"Well now, sir, I couldn't say as to why your donkeys paid a visit to Hunter's Hall. I expect you'd 'ave to ask the lady wot drove 'em there to find that out."

"A lady drove them there? When? And where is she?"

"When?" The tiger scratched his head. "Well now, sir, I'd say that would 'ave been about ten last evening. Give or take fifteen minutes 'ere and there. But as to where she is now" — he shrugged — "I couldn't say. All I heard was that she and me master drove off in a tearing hurry in his lordship's rig. And a finer equipage you'll never see. Pulled by the finest pair of 'orses since Noah 'ad the originals on the ark. Must 'ave been a fair treat for the lady after contemplating the arses of those miserable asses." He gave the donkeys a contemptuous look.

The last straining shred of Sir Edwin's patience snapped. He reached out and grabbed the tiger by the collar, lifting him up on his toes. "The devil take Lord Thornton's horses, and the devil take you! Now, give me a straight answer, or I'll shake you till your teeth rattle. Where were my sister and that loose screw going?"

The tiger was torn between terror for his life and the chance to torment the stiff-rumped toff further. He compromised with a more respectful tone and a tormenting truth. "I don't actually know where they was off to, sir, but I did 'ear, second 'and like, a mention of Gretna Green."

There was a stunned silence. Jocko almost forgot the death grip on his collar as he watched the toff's face go from fiery red to fish-belly white. He was not a malicious lad, merely mischievous. He had no desire to see the gentleman drop dead at his feet. So it was with considerable relief that he watched Sir Edwin release his grip and go staggering up the driveway toward his house.

The dazed gentleman was struggling to make sense of what he had just heard. Claudia run away with Lord Thornton? Ridiculous! That imp of Satan had to be lying. Why, Claudia had never even met the man. At least not to his knowledge. There was no need to put himself into any sort of taking until he actually discovered what was what. Chances were, it was all a hum. Claudia had never lacked for sense. Well, almost never. There was that one episode. Oh, God! With females one could never be sure of anything.

Discovering "what was what" proved difficult. His sister was not at home. And all his butler could tell him was that Miss Wentworth had rushed to the stables around nine the previous evening and ordered the donkeys harnessed and then driven off alone. "No, sir, she did not return." Nor had her bed been slept in. As for Miss Evelina, it was his understanding that she had gone to visit her friend Miss Seymore — and if Phillips had his own ideas on that subject, he felt it the better part of valor not to air them.

It was a grim-faced Sir Edwin who ordered his far-from-fresh horses and carriage to be brought out once again. The weary coachman did not have the luxury of revealing his thoughts when he was told to set out at once for Gretna Green.

Chapter Five

Relief had made Claudia ravenous. That and the fact she had eaten only tea and toast since reading Evelina's farewell note and setting off on this ramshackle odyssey. At another time The Crown's breakfast might have seemed inferior. But now the boiled eggs, cold ham, cold beef, light wigs, and marmalade were fit for the gods. She piled her plate high from platters set upon the round table before them and acknowledged Lord Thornton's mock amazement with a frosty set-down stare.

She did pause long enough to attempt a speech of gratitude to Lady Harville, who sat facing the doorway with Claudia on her left and his lordship on her right. But her ladyship would have none of it. "There will be time to do the pretty later, my dear. That is, if you insist upon it. But now let us relish the moment. We have routed the enemy and are entitled to an — err — feast."

She, too, appeared amazed at the quantity of food upon Miss Wentworth's plate. Claudia felt her face grow pink but pretended not to hear his lordship's chuckle.

He and his aunt, she noted, appeared to be the best of friends. They talked animatedly together. She soon stopped listening, for in the main, the conversation concerned the foibles of a variety of their relations. Instead she covertly watched the two young people, who had managed to put as much space between them as the circumference of the table would allow. Both pairs of eyes were downcast. Both faces were equally sullen. Both merely picked at their food. Claudia felt her own appetite begin to wane in the presence of so much hostility.

Thornton noticed. "Surely you are not quitting?" he asked politely as she laid down her fork. "I was on the point of ordering a roasted ox."

She did not dignify his banter with a reply.

"Pray overlook my nephew," Lady Harville sighed. "Most of the male Hunts are rag-mannered. It appears hereditary. In the same way some families produce left-handed progeny.

"Now, Rupert, if you will, go make sure the London stage has left. If so, we can make our departure."

He was back in a moment to report the coast was clear.

When she realized that Lady Harville was leading them toward her crested carriage, Claudia felt compelled to protest. "I would not dream of imposing upon your aunt any longer," she told Lord Thornton. "We should go directly home."

"That will prove difficult without transportation. I left my rig at Harville Hall. Besides, you heard my aunt tell your gossipy friend that you have come on a visit. Unless you spend some time there, you are bound to reactivate Mrs. Railton's tongue after all our efforts to still it."

"But I do not wish to impose," she repeated.

"Nonsense." Lady Harville had overheard and smiled back over her shoulder as her coachman handed her inside. "There is no imposition. I have no wish for this adventure to end. I have enjoyed it immensely. Add that to the reasons my nephew has given. I shall expect you to remain for at least a fortnight."

"But I am not prepared — it never occurred — I mean to say, I thought no further than the necessity to pursue." Claudia realized that not only was she babbling, she was causing extreme embarrassment to the elopers, both of whom seemed occupied with examining the cobblestones they stood upon. She tried again. "You see, I have brought no baggage. All I have with me is what I am wearing."

"Oh, that should present no problem."

To everyone's amazement, it was Rupert who spoke up. It was the first time he had uttered for ages, but his tone had not been softened by his silence.

"Evelina brought along a billion boxes. She could outfit an entire Ladies' Seminary."

Evelina jerked up her head to glare his way, a reaction he remained unaware of. "I admit I was chucklehead enough to prepare for a proper wedding journey. How could I have known that your idea of a honeymoon was a night in some Scottish croft?"

"Croft! Croft!" Rupert was indignant. "The Three Goslings is not a croft."

"Children! That will do." Her ladyship preempted the argument. "We should not keep the horses standing any longer."

Rupert was quick to spring to the coachman's box in case his brother had the same idea. It was obvious to all that he wished to be as far removed from Evelina as possible.

The other four settled themselves, with her ladyship and Lord Thornton facing forward and the Miss Wentworths opposite them.

Claudia had never ridden in such a well-sprung coach. It must be like riding on a magic carpet, she concluded, as they tooled effortlessly down the highway. She covertly stroked the creamy leather of the seats. Her eyes then strayed the short distance from her knees to where Lord Thornton sat slumped into a corner. His eyes were closed, his mouth slightly ajar.

"I have always envied gentlemen their ability to sleep under almost any circumstance," Lady Harville whispered. "It must be such a convenience."

"Yes, but he snores abominably."

Lady Harville looked startled.

Evelina gaped.

And Claudia felt her face grow red.

After a refreshing night's sleep, Claudia rose early. Lured by the vista she had admired from her window, she dressed quickly and found her way by trial and error through Harville Hall's maze of corridors. Her internal compass proved correct. There it was in the distance: an ornamental lake.

Except for pulling her cloak more closely around her, she was oblivious to the chill of the morning, for dew sparkled on the foliage, birds serenaded one another in the trees, and a peacock flaunted his exotic plumage to entice a nearby hen. She made her way toward the graveled path that encircled the man-made "natural" lake, which proved to be home to a wide assortment of waterfowl. A pair of black swans were the obvious majesties of the lot.

Claudia had had ample time to admire the domed gazebo situated upon a rise overlooking the lake before she drew abreast of it. She was considering leaving the path to sit a moment and enjoy the view when she realized that the small columned retreat was already occupied.

"Oh, Miss Wentworth!" Lady Harville's pleasant voice called out. "Do come and join me."

"Are you sure you wish to be disturbed?" Claudia asked as she entered the charming open structure and spied the book resting on her ladyship's lap.

"Positive. I brought along an improving volume, but find I much prefer to watch whatever Nature decides to offer up." She motioned Claudia to a seat beside her.

"I do see what you mean. As much as I enjoy reading, it could seem close to sacrilege on such a glorious morning. Are early walks your habit?"

"Rising early is my habit." Her ladyship wrinkled her nose in distaste. "It is one of the annoyances of age that one cannot sleep till all hours the way one did when young. But on a morning like this, it does seem more a blessing than a curse.

"But what of you, Miss Wentworth? I do hope the fact that you are abroad does not signify you have spent an uncomfortable night."

"Indeed not. My bed could not have been more comfortable. But it seemed unthinkable to waste a moment of my time here. I am loath to admit it, given the circumstances of our intrusion, but I find myself enjoying this adventure." She grimaced. "I fear that speaks volumes about the dullness of my life."

"Indeed?" Lady Harville studied her companion closely. "May I say that I find it most odd that a lovely young lady should be dull. You must be besieged with suitors."

"Hardly."

"Then, that gives me a very poor opinion of the gentlemen in your neighborhood."

"Thank you. But, in fact, mature eligible gentlemen are almost nonexistent in my neighborhood."

"Mature? Are you speaking of behavior? Then, perhaps you expect too much," her ladyship smiled. "And surely you cannot mean mature in years."

"Well, both, actually. You see, I am twenty-seven."

Lady Harville threw up her hands in pretended horror. "God bless us all! You are an ancient!"

Claudia laughed, but then turned serious. "You know quite well that at my age one is, in fact, past all romantic notions. Quite long in the tooth, as they say."

"Nonsense. I think it wonderful that more females do not postpone that fatal step until they reach the age of reason." She paused a moment to ponder what she had just said. "Not that one ever does reach that state, where the opposite sex is concerned. With a possible exception here and there. It does appear that your niece came to her senses just in time."

Claudia looked a bit doubtful. "I must say Evelina was eager to be rescued when Lord Thornton and I overtook them. I only pray that she will not have second thoughts. She lives in dread, you see, of winding up upon the shelf." She did not need to add "like me." The implication was obvious.

"That seems unlikely, for she is quite attractive, though by no means the diamond that you are."

Lady Harville's compliments were matter-of-fact. Flattery seemed foreign to her makeup.

"And," she continued the thought, "she certainly caused that young gudgeon Rupert to lose his head. But mayhap he, too, wished to avoid his elder's fate. For Thornton could be said to have set him a horrible example. Or at least it could be said if one applied the same standards to gentlemen as to ladies. But such a comparison is out of the question. Why is it that no one ever uses the phrase 'on the shelf' where men are concerned? Thornton must be several years older than you. In his thirties, I would say. Yet he is held up, not as an object of pity, but as a wily campaigner who has successfully escaped the lures of debutantes and the determination of their mamas for all these years."

Both ladies shook their heads in wonderment at this deplorable double standard.

"Indeed, the more I think on it," Lady Harville continued, "the more convinced I become that the wrong Hunt brother eloped. It is Thornton who should be hying off to Gretna Green. And" — her eyes glinted with determination — "I intend to see to it that he does. Not literally. For I do not approve of elopements unless there is no other recourse. But I do intend to see to it personally that he weds. My widowed sister is more likely to match-make for herself than for her sons — which could be a very good thing" — she smiled — "for she does not understand Thornton at all. As you can see, I have been giving the matter a great deal of thought. And I have the perfect young lady picked out for him."

"Indeed?" Claudia did her utmost to look enthusiastic. Doubtful was the best that she could manage.

"But does he not already have someone?"

"If he does," the other replied dryly, "he has kept her under wraps. What makes you think so?"

Claudia looked uncomfortable. "Well, on the drive north he let slip, you might say, someone's name. Perhaps you know her. Just who is Sophy?"

"Sophy?" Lady Harville frowned in thought. "Why, I have not the slightest idea."

Sir Edwin Wentworth's temper was testy at the best of times. Setting out in hot pursuit while still fatigued from a previous journey had not improved it. By the time he had reached The Crown, where he stopped to make inquiries, he had built up a head of steam that would have put Trevithick's new invention to the blush. And when he discovered that, indeed, the errant pair had spent the night in the inn, where they were accompanied by several of his lordship's family, instead of being relieved, the pressure built alarmingly.

How dare the Hunt family give their approval to this misalliance! Why, there had been bad blood between them and the Wentworths for generations. Well, he for one was having none of it. The pride of the Wentworths was not to be dismissed lightly. And if that jumped-up viscount thought that he could wed Sir Edwin Wentworth's sister in such a havey-cavey fashion, well, he would soon be relieved of that notion. Honor was at stake here. And no degree of rank — be it king or viscount — would be exempt from the just wrath of a wronged gentleman.

Sir Edwin's coach, drawn by fresh horses, reached the iron-pillared gateway to Lady Harville's estate in record time. The driveway appeared endless. But when it finally curved to afford a sight of Harville Hall, Sir Edwin refused to be overawed. The magnificence of the Jacobean pile simply rubbed more salt into his wounded pride. So they owned the earth, these kinfolk of Lord Thornton, did they? Well, Buck House itself — or even Windsor Castle — would not intimidate Sir Edwin Wentworth, whose ancestors had fought valiantly upon Bosworth Field.

When Lady Harville's butler ushered Sir Edwin into an entrance hall lavishly decorated with gilt and plasterwork, Lord Thornton was just coming down the curving staircase. His lordship was wearing a dark blue brocade dressing gown, a possession of the late Lord Harville, that left more of his bare limbs exposed than its designer had intended. His hair was tousled, his whiskers were making themselves visible again, and he was yawning prodigiously. Sir Edwin Wentworth saw red.

"You — you — libertine!" he shouted as he swept past the astonished butler with fists upraised. "You shall not get away with this, sir. Not while I live!" He flew at Lord Thornton like an errant whirlwind.

His lordship, who had reached the bottom of the steps and was wondering if he was really awake or indulging in some freakish nightmare, acted instinctively. No stranger to the boxing world, having stepped into the ring with a former world champion and acquitted himself quite credibly, he landed a facer that sent Sir Edwin sprawling upon the black-and-white-checkerboard marble like a toppled chessman. It was at this moment that Lady Harville and Miss Wentworth returned from their walk.

"Edwin!" Claudia gasped as she rushed to aid her brother, who was struggling to regain his feet. Dizziness forced him to scale back his ambitions. He settled for remaining seated upon the floor. He was having trouble keeping the enemy in focus, but he glared defiance nonetheless. Except for the red blood streaming from his nose, his face was chalky white. Claudia knelt beside him, trying ineffectively to staunch the flow with her wisp of a handkerchief while she followed his example with a better-directed glare.

"You could have killed him!" she accused.

"Don't stand there, Maxwell, go get some lint — bandages — water — whatever is required," Lady Harville snapped at her butler, who seemed transfixed.

Lord Thornton gave Miss Wentworth a jaundiced look. "I take it you know this madman. And as for killing him, I assume that was what he had in mind for me."

"Yes it was, you — you — libertine!" Once having settled upon the "mot juste," Sir Edwin was loath to let it go. His gorge was on the rise again now that the blood flow had subsided to a trickle. "And I will do it, by God! Just name your weapon."

"Edwin, do not be an ass!"

"You can name whatever you choose." The viscount was glaring daggers, which probably were not among the weapon possibilities. "But first would you mind telling me what this is all about?"

"What this is all about? What this is all about! Damn your eyes, you know perfectly well what this is all about."

"Sorry." Lord Thornton, despite his dishabille, was at his haughtiest. "I haven't the slightest notion."

"No notion!" Sir Edwin struggled to rise but was pushed back down by his sister. Two footmen had arrived with a basin of water, basilicum, and lint. They knelt beside the victim and began their ministrations. "You run off in the middle of the night with my sister as though she were some doxy and not a Wentworth of Fairwood Hall — a family of the first respectability, I will have you know — and you run off to Gretna Green as if she were some opera dancer. I doubt you ever intended to marry her!"

"Well, at least you are right on one count. Me, marry Miss Wentworth? The notion is absurd."

The object of this discussion ceased applying a

wet cloth to her brother's head. She raised her own to give his lordship a speaking look. He shrugged his shoulders, perhaps apologetically, then turned and stalked upstairs.

Chapter Six

Sir Edwin's condition improved with the departure of Lord Thornton and his brother, both of whom made it a point to avoid encountering the wounded baronet. That circumstance, plus a quantity of brandy, restored Sir Edwin's equilibrium enough for him to note his daughter's presence at Harville Hall and demand the reason why. Evelina's tearful explanation almost undid the soothing effects of both the absentees and the brandy.

His wrath now had two targets: Evelina, for her unforgivable breach of propriety, and Claudia, for her dereliction of duty. "My daughter should never have been allowed to become acquainted with a member of that family." He glared at his sister across the table in the sunny breakfast parlor, where Lady Harville had insisted that they gather.

"It is not Aunt's fault." Evelina spoke bravely through a mouthful of Sally Lunn. "I met Rupert quite by accident."

"Forgive my asking, Sir Edwin," Lady Harville intervened calmly to avert another tirade, "but could you enlighten me concerning the rift between the Wentworths and the Hunts? You see, I am only connected by marriage to *that family*." She diluted the venom he had applied to the term with a warm smile. "My sister married the late Lord Thornton, and if she ever spoke of any, err, unpleasantness, I fear I must not have been attending."

"Yes, Edwin, do explain." Claudia replenished her brother's teacup. "I must confess that I am not aware of the origins of the quarrel, either."

From the baronet's slight hesitation, it might have been deduced that he himself was not all that well steeped in family lore.

"Harrumph. Well, ah. As to which particular incident started the business, I cannot say. For there has been bad blood between the families for generations. I seem to recall my grandfather mentioning something about boundaries. And that the Hunts are not really entitled to the Abbey properties. It seems they bribed the magistrate to rule for them."

"When was this?"

"I cannot say precisely. Sometime in the sixteen hundreds, I collect."

"That long ago and we still —"

Sir Edwin frowned down his sister's look of incredulity. "In my opinion, the main offense of the Hunt family is their contemptible failure as stewards of their lands. They have never shown the slightest interest in the Yorkshire properties. For generations, their time has been spent on their estate in Kent or, more often than not, pleasure-seeking in London. They have only used Hunter's Hall on rare occasions to pursue the local game. In an effort to live up to their name, one supposes." He got no response to his feeble attempt at humor, and continued. "Though as for that, his present lordship has not made even that frivolous use of his holdings."

A vision of his present lordship's choice of frivolity flashed before Claudia's eyes. She quickly dispelled it. Interrupting a drunken card game was one piece of her history she was determined to forget.

"Such poor husbandry is unforgivable," her brother prosed on. "If a family cannot reside for at least a good part of the year upon its estate or if it feels itself too high in the instep for its neighbors, well, then, that family should sell to someone who would appreciate the property rather than allow it to go to rack and ruin."

"But all that is about to change, Papa. After Rupert was sent down from Oxford, you see, Lord Thornton decided that it would be a very good thing if he were to rusticate a bit and learn to manage the property. That is why he happened to be —" Evelina faltered and lowered her eyes back to her plate as she realized the folly of reopening her father's healing wounds. Lady Harville deftly changed the subject, and by the time Sir Edwin's carriage was announced, if he was not exactly in an easy state of mind, at least he was no longer choleric.

After the agreed-upon fortnight's visit, the two Wentworth ladies returned to Fairwood. They settled into an uneasy truce with the lord of the manor, whose first order of business had been to read them the riot act. They had sat side by side facing Sir Edwin across the library table with Evelina sniveling and Claudia reining in her temper as best she could. It helped not to listen too closely, but one could hardly miss all the references to "shocking impropriety" — of which sin both were guilty — and "besmirching the good name of Wentworth." But at last the tirade ended with an admonition that the episode never be spoken of again.

Claudia gladly agreed to this condition. Holding her tongue was no problem. She had no wish to discuss the business with either her brother or her niece. Her thoughts, though, were not as easily controlled.

For several days she fought hard against surrendering to the blue devils that lurked just below the surface of her mind. She had considered herself well beyond such fits of the dismals. She would have sworn she was now content with her lot. One might even say serene. Or perhaps "serene" was doing it too brown. "Resigned" might be the better term. But there was no denying that the shocking impropriety had upset her hard-won equilibrium. For when all was said and done, she, Claudia Wentworth, spinster, had had an adventure. For a brief interlude she had shed the passive for the active mode. And it had been glorious to feel alive again, to have gone tooling along the highway with a high-stepping pair of bloods under her control, with a man's head resting upon her shoulder.

"Stop it!" She stormed at her thoughts. No more of that. She had sworn never again to allow her fancy to travel that particular road. Far safer to recall the incredulous look in his lordship's fine eyes. "Me? Marry Miss Wentworth? The notion is absurd." There. That was better. Anger, she had discovered some time ago, is a marvelous anodyne.

So Claudia willed herself to look on the bright side. She had succeeded — well, to be fair, Lord Thornton had succeeded — in averting a scandal that would have ruined Evelina's life; however, there had been moments when the outcome seemed to lie in the balance. For when the Wentworth ladies first returned to Fairwood, Mrs. Railton had wasted no time in calling. As Claudia and she sipped their tea in the withdrawing room, Claudia could not help but conclude that the woman was wasted as a vicar's wife. The Spanish Inquisition would have been her proper milieu. The tiny eyes, lost though they were in the fleshy face, still succeeded in skewering one to one's chair as Mrs. Railton fed her insatiable curiosity. "How did you and Lady Harville become acquainted?" she probed.

Claudia was a devotee of truth, for practical as well as ethical reasons. Lies required a certain agility of mind that was difficult to maintain. She kept her replies as accurate as possible.

"Through correspondence, actually," she answered.

No falsehood here — not technically at any rate. For it was in an exchange of letters after the visit to Harville Hall that the two women had deepened their friendship. It became even more apparent that they shared the same liveliness of mind, the same appreciation of the absurd.

"And what did you think of Lord Thornton, Miss Wentworth?" the inquisitor continued.

"Why, there was little time to think of him at all," Claudia evaded. "He merely served as an escort to his aunt and left Harville Hall almost immediately."

"But surely you must have formed some opinion."

"Well, yes," she mused, "I collect that I did, fairly or unfairly. If you will not betray me to your husband for my lack of charity, Mrs. Railton, I will confess I found his lordship vain, spoiled, and entirely too high in the instep for my liking."

"Ah." Mrs. Railton digested this morsel of gossip with her seedcake. "I am not in the least amazed. Rackety, too, from what I hear. And his brother?"

"There I formed no impression whatsoever, for I saw even less of him than of Lord Thornton."

"I should suppose him to be of similar character."

"You are most likely right. Except, one must

recall that he is a second son, so he cannot be quite so proud as the firstborn, can he?"

"Well no," Mrs. Railton conceded, reluctantly, as she accepted another cup of tea. She took her leave soon afterward, hurrying off to share her newfound knowledge of the owner of Hunter's Hall with the other parishioners, leaving Claudia reasonably sure that Evelina's reputation was still intact.

Which was more than could be said for Evelina's disposition. The formerly lively, outgoing child-woman had turned into a recluse, avoiding her old friends and choosing to either snap or burst into tears whenever spoken to. Her sorely tried father attempted, unsuccessfully, to reason with her. Claudia, more sensitive to the girl's deep unhappiness, concluded that her best course was to ignore Evelina's vapors as far as possible and treat her normally. So when her niece interrupted her at her desk one early morning in May, she hastily stuffed her papers into a drawer and gave the girl an only partially forced smile.

There was no answering one. Quick to read Evelina's mercurial moods, Claudia saw that irritability was now in the ascendancy, preferable, perhaps, to despondency or despair.

"You surely cannot be writing to Lady Harville again so soon." Evelina frowned.

"No, as a matter of fact."

"Good. For the postman has just called, and here is another letter from her to you. It would not do to get out of turn."

She plopped the folded missive upon the desk, then flounced across the room to sink down upon a window seat and stare out at the spring rain. "I really do not see what you two can find to say to one another," she remarked in the direction of the window. "Why, she is old enough to be your mother."

"Separation of generations does not necessarily dampen communication," Claudia replied patiently as she broke the seal and began to scan the contents.

"You sound like an improving sampler. I must say that you never used to be so prosy."

Claudia was not listening. "Oh, my goodness!" She stared at the letter as though her eyes were playing tricks.

Her shock secured Evelina's full attention. The girl wheeled around, and for once forgot her pose. "What is it? Is something wrong?"

"Wrong? No, not at all. At least not precisely. Though I greatly fear that Edwin will never permit it."

"Never permit what?" Evelina jumped up from the window seat and hurried across the room to peer over her aunt's shoulder at the crossed letter, written both vertically and horizontally on the page to save the recipient from paying extra postage. "Can you actually read that?" She squinted hard, then gave up in disgust. "What on earth has she said to put you in such a taking?"

"It is an invitation." Claudia's voice rose with excitement. "To you and me. Lady Harville wishes us to visit her in London."

Chapter Seven

"You cannot imagine the excitement," Lady Harville had written from her house in town. "The city is wild with joy. At last that monster, Napoleon, is defeated. This horrid, tedious war is finally at an end. All the allied leaders will be here to celebrate. The czar's sister, the Grand Duchess Catherine of Oldenburg, is already ensconced in Pulteney's Hotel. The *on dit* is that she and the Prince Regent are at daggers drawn — but more of that when I see you. There is enough delicious gossip circulating to sate even your Mrs. Railton. You and your niece must come."

Here, Claudia stopped reading aloud. She thought it tactful not to let Evelina know how much she had revealed to her new friend.

"I can guarantee," the letter continued, "that it will be impossible for Evelina to remain in the mopes in the midst of all this excitement. And if her father is concerned about Rupert Hunt, he need not be. The popular song of the moment is 'All the World's in Paris' — not that you would know it from our crowded streets. It seems to me that 'all the world's' in London. But they do say there are twelve thousand British visitors there. Now it is twelve thousand and one, including Rupert. All I can say is, those tourists have no notion of what they are missing here. So you must join me as soon as possible. I need someone to laugh with at all our ridiculous excesses. And I command you to bring your manuscript along."

The invitation's effect upon Evelina was instantaneous. Her eyes sparkled. She actually smiled, though her aunt would have sworn that the facial muscles required for this exercise had long since atrophied. The transformation was, alas, short-lived. "Papa will never permit it," she sighed as her expression reverted to type.

"Then, we must persuade him." Claudia's voice held a great deal more resolution than she felt.

But in actuality, overcoming Edwin's objections was much easier than expected. For one thing, he was delighted, though he would never admit it even to himself, to have his family upon such intimate terms with such an important member of the ton. For another, he had had his fill of Evelina's moods. And when his sister pointed out that there was no danger of any contact with the Honorable Rupert, the matter was settled. They would leave for London in two days' time.

Their arrival in the Metropolis coincided with the morning parade of the Horse Guards from their barracks to Hyde Park. As the cymbals clashed and the drums pounded, it was difficult for Claudia and Evelina to believe that such pomp and circumstance was not meant for them.

And when their coach drew up before the grandest house in fashionable Grosvenor Square, it was even harder to believe that Lady Harville was not actually the fairy godmother of every young girl's dreams.

Indeed, in the days that followed, her ladyship fitted that role. The ideal hostess, she provided for each guest's entertainment separately, catering to their individual tastes. "You have not come to London to play duenna to your niece," she lectured Claudia, rightly guessing that Sir Edwin's orders had been to do just that. Since Evelina was not yet out, her activities were of course circumscribed. But her hostess had arranged for an introduction into a set of young people, where "she will be as well chaperoned as even your stickler of a brother would require." And Evelina was soon caught up in a whirlwind of picnics, parties, and sight-seeing trips that brought the roses back into her cheeks and led her to declare that London life was "too, too famous for words."

As for Claudia, Lady Harville was determined that she have time to pursue her own interests without being monopolized by "one of the antiques Lord Elgin overlooked."

"But that is absurd. You are not an antique. Why, you are younger than I in outlook, if not in years."

This conversation took place immediately upon the Wentworths' arrival as the two friends sipped tea in Harville House's smaller, silk-lined withdrawing room. Evelina had gone off with a maid "to supervise the unpacking," which in actuality meant to lean out her bedchamber window as far as possible and gawk at the sights of Grosvenor Square.

Lady Harville gave Claudia a level stare over her Wedgwood cup. "Well, if that is so, your outlook is in need of stimulation. You must allow me to introduce you to the theater and to the opera."

"Oh, I should like that above all things."

"And to some young people."

Claudia's enthusiasm suffered a dampening. "If you will forgive me, I have no desire to cultivate the acquaintance of 'young people.' I am rather beyond all that."

"You may no longer be a member of the infantry, my dear, but you are still young. Besides, one should not be beyond friendship at any age."

"Friendship?" Claudia's eyebrows rose. "What makes me believe it is matchmaking you have in mind?"

"What an appalling idea." Her hostess raised her arms in protest. "I would never consider such a thing. I loathe females who meddle in matters of the heart. That is my only consolation for never having had a daughter. I should have hated having to hawk her in the marriage market like some gypsy's wares. No, my dear, put yourself at ease. I am above such vulgarity. I never matchmake."

The younger woman laughed. "What a whisker! You have already declared your intention of maneuvering your nephew into marriage."

"Oh, well, that." Lady Harville waved her hand dismissively. "That is not the same thing at all."

"And pray, why not?"

"I do not consider getting Thornton leg-shackled 'matchmaking.' 'Wild game hunting' would be a better term. I long to see him trapped and caged."

"What a terrible analogy."

"Yes, isn't it." Lady Harville smiled wickedly. "But you may rest easy. I have no designs upon your future. I find your own plans far more exciting. Conventionality leaves much to be desired. Now, tell me. Have you finished? And did you bring it? Ah, you are fairly squirming in your chair, I see. Confess, my dear. How many times have you cursed yourself for confiding in me? No, no. Don't bother to deny it. You are certain to have done so."

Claudia smiled a sheepish smile. "Well, it is true that you have a way of inspiring confidences that one had not thought to reveal. I have always kept my — pastime — secret."

"I realize as much. And I wonder why."

"Because, when I look at the thing objectively —"

"Always a mistake," the other murmured.

"It seems absurd — and arrogant — to think that I could take my place along with the likes of Maria Edgeworth and Fanny Burney."

"But when you look with your heart?"

"One's heart is never the best judge of anything."

"Indeed? Well, perhaps you are right. That is why I am prepared to be your judge and jury. As I said when we first became acquainted, I consider my literary taste to be superior. I will read your novel and give you my honest opinion as to its suitability for publication."

"At the risk of our friendship?" The laugh was rather forced.

"Oh, I consider you far too sensible to let our friendship die over an unfavorable review. I collect you will only be out of charity with me for four or five years. Or only one or two if I am tactful."

"Now, then." She deftly closed that subject. "About your plans for seeing everything there is to see in London. Here is a Bible for you." She fished in the workbasket by her chair and produced a London guide. "I refuse to accompany you, you understand. I shall save my strength for the finer things, like the Theatre Royal."

Claudia accepted the guide gratefully and wasted little time in rising to its challenge. In a remarkably short period, she had crossed off the Tower, the British Museum, the Royal Academy, Westminster Abbey, and St. Paul's. But her favorite recreation was to set out on foot, with or without maid or footman, depending upon where Lady Harville's attention was at the time, and explore. She was most fascinated by the variety of shops catering to the needs and whims of

Mayfair: tailors, milliners, perfumers, jewelers, chemists, umbrella and parasol makers, cheesemongers, grocers, tea and coffee merchants, linen and woolen drapers — the list was endless. She roamed for hours, buying little, but often resolving to come back just before their return to Yorkshire and take advantage of certain bargains she had spied.

On one such expedition, she had spent a pleasant hour in Wedgwood and Byerley's Warehouse on St. James's Square and was seriously considering choosing a complete new set of china for Fairwood, even though Edwin would consider it a frivolous waste of money. She selected a teapot from one of the several large, round tables where wares were displayed and carried it over to a floor-to-ceiling window in order to take advantage of the better light. She was holding it aloft and rotating it slowly, admiring the white Grecian designs that stood out in bas-relief against the powder blue and trying to recall from her school days the mythology they represented, when a throat cleared right behind her. She looked back over her shoulder and promptly dropped the pot.

"Oh, my horrors!" she gasped.

"And it is very nice to see you, too, Miss Wentworth."

Lord Thornton swept off his curly-brimmed beaver and bowed mockingly.

Chapter Eight

The hum of business stopped. All eyes were turned their way. Claudia's instinctive reaction was to go down upon her knees and begin to gather up the pieces of shattered china. Her face was hot.

"I hardly think it necessary for you to bother with that." Lord Thornton stood over her with folded arms and what should have been an impassive expression. His eyes betrayed him. They glinted with amusement. He offered a gloved hand and tugged her to her feet just as an apron-clad youngster carrying a broom arrived.

Words failed her.

"Damnation?" he supplied.

"Exactly."

Diligent sweeping began about their feet.

"Since you do not strike me as the clumsy sort, I must assume that the sight of me came as a shock."

At the moment the sight of him, dapper in high collar, intricate cravat, white waistcoat with yellow trim, bottle green long-tailed coat, fawn-colored tight-fitting flattering pantaloons tucked into gleaming boots, every inch, in fact, the Bond Street beau, was having a decidedly unsettling effect, the most definable part of which was to make her feel countrified in her Yorkshire-made gray pelisse and cornette bonnet. She got a tighter grip upon her poise.

"Well, you are the last person I should have" — she hesitated — "expected to see."

"Wished to see, you mean? I do live in London, you know. You might have realized there was some risk of encounter."

"If I had given the matter thought — which I did not —" she lied, "I should certainly not have expected an encounter in a china shop."

"Bulls only?" He was fishing in his pocket and produced a card that he handed to the officious clerk, who had borne down upon them. It worked like magic. Officious turned to fawning. "Send me the bill for the wreckage."

"No!"

Claudia began digging in her cluttered reticule. Lord Thornton took her firmly by the arm and bade the bowing clerk good day.

"I cannot allow you to pay for my carelessness," she fumed as he steered her out into the street.

"Then, I won't pay." He grinned. "It will not be the first bill I have contrived to overlook."

"That being the case, I shall return and settle the thing right now." She made an attempt to do so, but the grip on her arm tightened.

"Oh, well, then. If it hurts your puritan conscience, I promise to settle with Wedgwood and Byerley. Satisfied?"

"Not really. It puts me even further in your debt."

"How galling."

"Well, yes, as a matter of fact, it is."

"But think what it does for my self-esteem. Why, I am beginning to feel like a knight-errant, always rescuing you from this and that. And pray don't start that again! Are you trying to give carte blanche to the pickpockets?"

She was struggling with the contents of her reticule as they turned onto Piccadilly and jostled through the crowds.

"I am trying to pay you for that curst teapot."

"Very well, then, if you must discharge your debt — an attitude that will mark you as a complete flat in London, by the by — you can begin by buying us coffee."

"I hardly think that would be the thing. Even in London."

"In that case I will pay."

"That is not what I meant, and you know it."

"Do I? No need to look so outraged. I was not suggesting a coffeehouse. Or anything else the least bit shocking."

"You weren't?" Her voice was skeptical.

"No, indeed. Word of a gentleman. The place I have in mind would not raise even Mrs. Railton's eyebrows. Well, perhaps that is doing it a bit too brown. Forget Mrs. Railton, but take my word, every visitor to London should see the White Horse Cellar. For that matter, most do see it, for it is the main point of arrival from the West. Of people and mail."

"The White Horse Cellar," she mused. "I am sure I have heard of it. A coaching office?"

"Yes, indeed. Of the utmost respectability. Where else would you and I seek refreshment? We shall blend right in. A gentleman and his mother departing for Bath." He laughed at her glare. "Oh, very well. A gentleman and his aunt, then. By the by, may I say that you do hide your advanced years well?"

She rose to bait. "They are not all that advanced, and it is certainly rag-mannered of you to say it."

"Me? I would not have dreamt that you are ancient. It was your niece who let the world know you are ready for a Bath chair."

"My niece, as you should recall, is not yet sixteen. I do not doubt that she considers even you antiquated."

"She is bound to do so" — he grinned — "since I am actually three years older than you. By the by, how are your feet holding out?" He was most solicitous.

"Very well, thank you. And yours?" She looked down at his boots, made for him by Hoby most likely. No problem there, obviously.

"Oh, I think I can totter on to our destination. We are almost there." They were turning into Arlington Street. "Green Park is just a stone's throw from here," he declaimed with an expansive gesture and a guide-to-visitor's voice. "Been there?"

"No. I have been to Hyde Park, though."

"Oh, well, then. If you have seen one park, you have seen —"

"It is not that I begrudge you your amusement at my expense, but it does miss the mark by a mile. I fully intend to visit Green Park. There simply has not been time. Oh, my!"

They were passing through the arches into the inn yard. Nothing in her limited experience with coaching houses had prepared her for this scene.

"Startling, isn't it?" her escort observed.

"Why, one would think it was a fair."

There were purveyors of goods everywhere, loudly hawking their wares: oranges, pencils, sponges, cakes — anything that a traveler or a stay-at-home spectator (for this category far outnumbered the other) might need to lighten a journey or serve as a souvenir. Lord Thornton elbowed their way through the throng, ignoring the insistent peddlers imploring him to buy.

As they entered the travelers' room, Claudia paused to gaze around her. "I must say I expected better," she commented sotto voce.

"Why?"

"Well, this *is* the Metropolis, and the inn *is* famous and all, but it really is no better furnished than The Crown."

"You can't fault the attention, though," he murmured back as a weary-looking waiter in a dirty apron materialized to guide them to one of the hard-benched cubicles that divided the room.

"Coffee?" Thornton inquired as they took their seats, and Claudia nodded. "And bring us some buns as well.

"They are surprisingly good here," he assured

her as the waiter drifted away.

There was a moment's uncomfortable silence while Claudia gazed around to avoid looking across the table.

"You seem rather awestruck, Miss Wentworth. And I had thought you unimpressed with the White Horse."

"Awestruck? Certainly not. Astounded, perhaps. And if so, it has nothing to do with the posting house. To speak plainly, I cannot imagine why I am sitting here with you."

"Why, to repay me for that shattered teapot, of course," he replied as the waiter reappeared with their refreshment. "What a shockingly short memory you have.

"Give the bill to the lady," he instructed as the man distributed the cups, saucers, plates, cream, sugar, and buns. The waiter's head jerked up, and he shot his lordship a scornful look.

"Well, that's sunk me." Thornton gazed sorrowfully at the retreating back while Claudia laughed in spite of herself.

"You really are incorrigible."

"Not incorrigible, considerate. My objective is to put you at your ease. For you are galled at the thought of being beholden to me. You might as well admit it."

"Well, yes. But there were more delicate ways — Oh, never mind."

"I agree." He passed her the buns. "Let us change the subject. We certainly have many more interesting ones to choose."

"We have?" She appeared to wrack her brain. "Sorry, I am unable to come up with a single topic."

"Oh, come now. You cannot have forgot our history so soon. Wild rides through the night in hot pursuit of eloping halflings, a harrowing encounter with a character assassin in a posting house, an assault upon my person at Harville Hall —"

"An assault upon *your* person?" she interrupted. "As I recall, it was my brother who was stretched out upon the floor with a bloodied nose while you remained unscathed."

"That is your embroidered version. Go on, eat your bun. It could improve your memory."

Exercise, Claudia discovered, had made her ravenous. And he was right; the buns were delicious.

"Should I guard my share?" he inquired. "I am remembering your, err, healthy appetite in The Crown. Is there something about coaching houses that makes you peckish? I must say I am astounded by your girlish figure. I should think —"

"Lord Thornton, if you think to shame me out of my share, you waste your time." She took a second.

"Oh, well," he sighed. "I should remember. You *are* paying for them.

"Tell me, what brings you to London?" he asked as he deftly palmed the last bun on the plate.

"Isn't it obvious? My niece and I are no different from the rest of that mob." She gestured vaguely in the direction of the street. "We wish to celebrate the end of the war. And, as I expect you know, your aunt was kind enough to invite us here."

"Was she, indeed? You've become bosom bows, have you? Actually, I am not acquainted with her activities. For to be quite candid, I have been avoiding my aunt of late."

"Indeed? I had thought you on the best of terms. Don't tell me you have quarreled."

"No, no," he hastened to reassure her. "Nothing like that. It is just that she is quite determined to find me a wife. Has in fact become quite a bore on the subject. So I find it more comfortable to avoid her. Oh, good God!" He broke off to stare at Claudia speculatively. "You don't imagine that she —"

"No, I do not!" she snapped. "Lady Harville does not want for sense. Besides, even if she could have ever entertained such a sapskulled notion — which I assure you she would not have done — you have made yourself quite clear on that subject."

The blue eyes widened. "I have?"

"You certainly have. After my brother accused you of eloping with me, you were at some pains to point out the absurdity of the notion."

"Oh, well." He shrugged and smiled apologetically. "The heat of the moment and all that. I certainly did not intend offense."

"And none was taken," she replied, a bit, perhaps, too starchily. "For I quite agree.

"But it does seem to me" — she veered the conversation away from the personal — "that if Lady Harville's matchmaking bothers you, you should simply tell her that your interest is already fixed."

"I beg your pardon?"

"You heard me."

"Heard, but failed to understand. You wish me to lie to my sainted aunt?" He took a large bite of bun.

"No, of course not. You should simply tell her about Sophy."

His lordship choked.

Chapter Nine

It took Thornton some time to recover. Claudia was considering thumping him on the back when he finally managed to speak.

"S-Sophy? Who the devil told you about Sophy?"

"Why, you did. In a manner of speaking."

"Never!"

"Not intentionally. But you did mention her name in your sleep."

He would have choked again, but he lacked the means.

"Good God! Whenever did I — we — ?"

"You might remember that you fell asleep in the barouche." Her tone was, to say the least, repressive.

"Did I? Well, that is certainly a relief. Tell me, how is your niece faring these days?"

The abrupt change of subject was hardly subtle. He could just as well have told her to mind her own business, Claudia thought, for he'd no intention of discussing Sophy with her. Indeed, at the moment he seemed to consider her a soul mate of Mrs. Railton. "Evelina is enjoying London very much," she replied with an excess of polite formality.

"Oh, is she indeed?" He took a restoring sip of coffee. "That puts my poor brother in his place."

"Oh, I doubt he is suffering any heartburnings in Paris."

"Who knows? Rupert is young. And sensitive. And your niece did trample upon his sensibilities with hobnailed boots. And males are not as quick to slough off blighted romances as females are."

"Rubbish!" So much for polite formality.

"You disagree? Then, let me observe that your niece is a case in point. She appears to have sloughed off Rupert in record time. Callous, I'd call it."

"Callous has nothing to say in the matter. She is only fifteen, for heaven's sake. And she did not 'slough off' anything. She was quite impossible to live with if you must know."

"Weep a lot did she?" He grinned.

"As a matter of fact, she did. And I see nothing amusing about it."

"Nor do I," he retorted. "In fact, as I pointed out to him, Rupert appears to have had a fortunate escape. It could grow rather wearing to be married to a fountain. Did her parents consider christening her Niobe? After the Greek weeper that Hamlet —"

"Don't bother to explain. 'Like Niobe, all tears.' I have been to school, too, Lord Thornton. But Evelina is not like that at all in the normal way. And now that Lady Harville has made her acquainted with a circle of young people, she is becoming cheerful once again. Quite her old self, in fact."

"I am very glad to hear it. For I suspect that underneath all that moisture lies a pretty face. Looks a bit like you, doesn't she? Only more vapid."

"You are quite determined to be offensive about her, are you not?"

"Put it down to male pride. I hated to see my brother's heart broken."

"Fustian. He was even more relieved than Evelina to be rescued from the altar."

"Oh, well, you win," he conceded. "And, actually, I have not taken against your weepy niece. I merely enjoy watching your hackles rise. See, there they go again."

"And I intend to rise with them." She stood. "Your aunt will wonder what has become of me."

The hovering waiter materialized and attempted to present his lordship with a bill. Thornton deliberately folded his arms across his chest while Claudia fumbled in her reticule for the proper coins. The waiter looked on with scorn. As they left the inn, her face was flushed with embarrassment.

Not only had the city crowds increased, they discovered as they passed back through the inn-yard arches, but everyone seemed in a rush that bordered upon panic. Indeed, quite a few of the younger able-bodied folk were running.

"Is something on fire?" Claudia gasped as a loping youth almost sent her sprawling.

His lordship threw a protective arm around her. "Not likely," he answered for the lad who had merely mumbled, "Beg pardon, miss," and shown his heels. "It most probably means that some of our distinguished visitors have gone abroad. This sort of thing happens every time one of them sticks a nose out of his quarters. Instant mobs collect and follow. There really should be some sort of ordinance. For the health and safety of the citizenry. If this continues, half the population is bound to trample the other half."

"You're bamming me, are you not?"

She was forced to crane her neck to look up at him. Goodness, he was tall. She knew she should extricate herself from the encircling arm, but just as she was making a move to do so, a puffing fat man brushed by and his lordship drew her closer. The action was quite gentlemanly under the circumstances, her inner voice conceded.

"No, I am perfectly serious," he was saying. "This happens constantly. I expect that the czar and his sister are to blame this time. We are not far from Pulteney's Hotel, where they are staying. I have heard that they take walks about this time every day." They were turning into Piccadilly and were swept up by a frenzy of pedestrians. "I should have remembered and chosen another route."

"Another route?" Claudia's eyes were sparkling. "Are you mad? I wish to see them."

She broke free of his protective arm, its comfort quite forgot, hitched up her skirts a bit, and joined the group that was sprinting down the street in the direction of the park.

"Hey, wait!" His lordship, dumbstruck momentarily by her unexpected action, collected his wits and hurried after her. "Tourists!" he muttered scathingly as he came abreast and grabbed her gloved hand. "Determined to be trampled, are you?"

"No, to trample." She laughed up at him.

The crowd halted suddenly, then broke into huzzahs. Thornton elbowed a way through the mob till they were standing next to the street. He placed Claudia in front of him and served as a buffer against the pressing crowd.

"See," he said in her ear, "I was right about the celebrities. It is Alexander and the grand duchess. But I had the means of locomotion wrong."

The czar and his sister were riding in an open carriage with a military escort fore and aft. The royal pair appeared oblivious to the cheering throng. The Grand Duchess Catherine, described by Lord Clancarty as "the czar's platter-faced sister," stared stonily ahead while, opposite her, the czar of all the Russias engaged in earnest conversation with the young British officer beside him.

Claudia had quite forgot herself and was cheering as lustily as anyone while Thornton watched indulgently. Then suddenly she gasped and, reaching back, clutched his arm for support.

"Miss Wentworth, what is it?"

Her eyes were riveted upon the carriage. All

the color had drained from her face. "Are you all right?" he asked anxiously. "Good Lord, you aren't about to faint now, are you?"

She did not answer. Her eyes remained glued upon the carriage as it made its stately way past them and on down the mob-lined street.

After reassuring himself that his companion was not about to swoon, Thornton followed the direction of her gaze with narrowed eyes until the coach had passed out of their view.

The crowd followed after it. They remained standing in their hard-won place alone.

"Are you all right?"

"Oh, certainly." Her color was gradually returning. She did her best to sound offhand, though her voice was a bit too shaky for conviction. "I confess I felt a bit faint there just for a moment. Due to all the excitement, I collect. I do beg pardon. I am not normally so missish."

"No, I never took you for the vaporish sort." They began to walk away slowly, both deep in thought.

Thornton broke their silence. "Pretty, ain't he?"

She emerged from her reverie with difficulty. "The czar? Well, he is generally considered handsome, I am told. But it is difficult for me to judge."

"No, not the czar. The English cove who was with him. The one that put you into such a taking."

"Whatever do you mean? No one put me in a

87

taking. You much mistake the matter."

Her repressive tone put a period to the conversation.

He shrugged slightly, and they continued to walk in silence toward Grosvenor Square.

Chapter Ten

After leaving Claudia at Lady Harville's door, Thornton automatically headed for St. James's Street. But then, instead of entering White's Club for Gentlemen, his usual haunt, he crossed the street to a rather modest-looking residence that housed the Guard's Club. This association had only recently been established under the auspices of the Prince Regent and the Duke of Wellington. His Royal Highness and the military hero had agreed that the officers returning from Spain needed somewhere to go that would not be as expensive as the more fashionable clubs or as sordid as the taprooms and chop houses that were their alternatives.

After a word to the club doorman, Thornton went inside. It took him only a moment to locate his quarry in the library. Colonel Dan McKinney, small and wiry with a deep scar on his forehead that betrayed his profession, was sprawled in a soft leather chair, reading the *Times*. An empty glass stood on a small table near his elbow. He looked up as Thornton approached, and whooped a greeting. "Thorn! You old reprobate! What are you doing on this side of the street, slumming?"

"Looking for you, actually." Thornton sank down in the twin to the colonel's chair.

"Done up, are you, and in need of a loan?" The colonel, whose pockets were always to let due to his love of and lack of skill in gaming, gave his affluent friend an impish grin. "First we'll have a spot of something to loosen up me purse." He waved at a waiter, who, anticipating such a signal, was already halfway to their table. "Another of the same." He nodded toward the empty glass. "And you, Thornton?"

"Coffee."

"Milksop! Can't abide associating with civilians." He smiled affably. "So tell me, what brings you here? And don't say it's the pleasure of my company."

"Oh, God, no. Got my fill of that in school," the other grinned. "What I want is information."

"From me? And I always thought you were the knowing one."

"Well, this should be your area of expertise. You've been involved in herding our royal visitors from place to place, haven't you?"

"For me sins, yes," the other groaned. They waited for the waiter to serve their drinks and leave.

"You see, I — and roughly three-quarters of the London population, I would guess — watched the czar and his sister ride down Piccadilly just a bit ago."

"My word, man, can't you find anything better to do than ogle those puffed-up foreigners? Waste of anyone's time I can tell you, for a more stiff-rumped cove than that curst Russian ain't imaginable. Tells you something that I even feel sorry for our coxcomb of a Regent having to do the polite with that royal pain. And his sister's even worse. Did you know that she had the gall to stop the music being played in her honor at the guild hall? Doesn't like music of any sort. What a thornback!"

"It's not the Russians that I'm interested in." Thornton interrupted what was fast turning into a tirade.

"Well, that shows taste on your part."

"There was a Guardsman in the carriage with them. Wondered if you could identify the cove."

The colonel's eyes were narrowing. "Most like I can. But go on and describe him anyhow."

"Handsome."

McKinney snorted.

"At least women would find him so I should think. Fair-haired Adonis type."

"Say no more. Bound to have been Major Hugo Landseer. He's always to be found in the Russians' pockets."

"Indeed? And who exactly is he?"

"Nobody, I'd say. Except that he is one of those coves determined to get on in the world with an eye always fixed on the best chance."

"Like chumming with the czar?"

"Oh, much more than chumming. You sell the fellow short. He's connected with Alexander by marriage."

"Indeed?" Thornton's eyebrows elevated. "Married, is he?"

The colonel took a long swallow from his glass and settled in to gossip. "Married to a cousin, or some such thing, of the czar. Met her in Spain. Her father's a diplomat posted there. She bears a striking resemblance to the grand duchess, by the by. Every bit as platter-faced. And she's still young."

"Indeed? Well, he's pretty enough for the two of them. Is she here in London?"

"Lord, no. He left her behind. Might have done anyway, but the excuse is she's breeding." He paused to chuckle wickedly. "For the second time."

Thornton waited.

"The first time created quite a stir, let me tell you. Happened without benefit of clergy."

"A state of affairs not too uncommon."

"True. But in this particular case it almost caused an international incident. It was said that her father came close to shooting the pretty major. But in the end he came to his senses and had 'em legshackled instead. Though they say it fair near killed him."

"Hmmm." Thornton mulled the information over. "Call me an Anglophile if you like, but I fail to see how an English gentleman could be so far beneath her touch. From your description of her beauty — or lack thereof — she could not have been a prime commodity on the marriage mart."

"Oh, you think not? She's an only child, and her father's fortune, they say, runs a close second to the czar's. Old Croesus ain't even in the running with the Russian. Besides, it was common knowledge what had happened. Landseer deliberately seduced her with an eye less on her than on her inheritance. Doubt the poor widgeon had the faintest notion of what was what. At least that was the story spread by those close to the situation. She'd been sheltered like a hothouse plant. Most likely thought that babies were left under cabbage leaves by the fairies till Landseer came along and showed her a better way.

"There now, you've pumped me dry. It's your turn. Are you going to tell me why you want Major Landseer's history?" He paused expectantly, then shook his head in mock disgust. "I didn't think so. You always were a downy cove, Thorn."

They switched the subject and chattered a few more minutes, but it was obvious that Thornton's mind was not really focused upon the whereabouts of old school chums. He was still preoccupied as he left the Guard's Club and, ignoring beckoning friends in the bow window of White's, turned toward home.

Claudia had been able to enter the town house unobserved. She went directly to her chamber, and after removing her shoes and bonnet, collapsed upon the canopied bed. She felt the beginning of a headache. Her hand shook as she picked up a book from the bedside table, then, realizing the futility of such a gesture, put it back again.

What was it that Lord Thornton had said? He had never taken her for the vaporish sort? Nor had she. She would not have dreamt that the sight of Hugo could undo her in this fashion. She had believed herself well beyond such feelings. Was she not, in fact, fashioning another kind of life?

Indeed she was! And she would not languish like some spineless gothic heroine.

Claudia rose from the bed and crossed the room with grim determination. She sat down at a satinwood writing desk that Lady Harville had had moved into the French-style chamber for her convenience. Resolutely she pulled out paper from a drawer, then dipped her pen into the well with an excess of determination. The first evidence of creativity was an inkblot.

It was also the last. Claudia stared as it spread out on the paper, forming what? A toad? No, a pot? A crocodile? This was ridiculous. Writing was always her escape from harsh reality. Now no words would come. And between her and the crocodile? — the map of Italy? — whatever — there was another image she could not get rid of: classic features; softly curling flaxen hair; light blue eyes, tender and smiling, fringed with incredibly thick dark lashes.

"Stop it! This is ridiculous," she muttered, crumpling up the blotted paper and hurling it across the room, then going to pick it up again. And since she had set herself in motion, continuing seemed the only sensible course. Exercise could help. As if she had not already tramped over half of London. Nonetheless, she began to march around and around the blue-and-white-striped room while the headache gained momentum.

The walls of Harville House were thick, but not quite thick enough. For as she passed her door for the fifteenth time, she heard someone running down the corridor. The door to the chamber next to hers, occupied by Evelina, slammed. Brief silence was followed by a storm of weeping.

Well, it was that sort of day. Claudia ceased her exercise to listen. Then, when the storm showed no signs of abating, she sighed and went to see what the matter was.

"C-come in."

The voice that had answered her knock was muffled. Well, no wonder. She discovered Evelina lying facedown upon her bed, her body shaking with the force of her sobs. "Like Niobe, all tears" rose unbidden to her mind, and she could have kicked Lord Thornton for planting an image she might never get rid of.

"Evelina, dear," Claudia murmured sympathetically as she sat down upon her niece's bed and laid a comforting hand upon her shoulder, "whatever is the matter?"

The sobs increased.

"Come, dear," she coaxed, "tell me. Perhaps I can help."

"N-no one can h-help me" was the convulsed reply.

No doubt she was right, Claudia silently agreed. That was usually the way. Still, one could only try.

"Tell me anyhow," she said gently, stroking the heaving back.

"Oh, Claudia, he's here! He is actually here in London."

The stroking ceased as the stroker stiffened. "Yes," she finally managed. "I know."

Evelina whirled upright to a sitting position. Her tear-stained face contorted with fury.

"You knew? And you did not tell me? That — that — is despicable!"

"Just one minute, young lady," Claudia snapped back. "I do not care for your tone. And I could not possibly have told you, for I only just discovered the fact myself. Not that I would necessarily have mentioned it. Indeed, I most likely would not have done, since I cannot see how you are in any way concerned."

"Not concerned!" Evelina erupted. "Not concerned! How can you say such a thing?"

Claudia was beginning to wonder the same thing herself. "Evelina," she said slowly, "what are we talking about?"

"Rupert, you lobcock! We are talking about Rupert!"

"Oh, my heavens! I did not realize. What you must have thought. Pray forgive me."

Evelina looked partially mollified. And slightly curious. "But what on earth did you think I was talking about?"

"Never mind. It was not important. But are you sure?"

"Of course I am sure. I could hardly confuse Rupert Hunt with someone else, now, could I? The Duke of Wellington, for instance." Her hysteria was rapidly returning.

"I am sorry. That was a sapskulled thing to say. Suppose you simply tell me just how you came to see him."

"Oh, Claudia, it was horrible." Fresh tears welled. Moved by what was obviously a genuine distress, Claudia clucked sympathetically and handed over her handkerchief. Evelina blew her nose and continued. "Caroline Webster's mother had arranged this picnic, you remember."

Claudia nodded.

"We all met at her house. Everyone was there. The Whitfield sisters, George Locke, Harry Williams — you know, all the usual crowd."

Again a confirming nod.

"And Caroline said, 'I think you know everyone else, Miss Wentworth, but allow me to present Mr. Hunt.'"

"Oh, my."

"And there he was, looking just the same only his face was browned by the sun. And he s-said, 'How do you do — Miss Wentworth, is it?' And he was looking at me as though I were a p-perfect stranger that he had never seen before in his life."

"Oh dear. How awful for you. Still, though,"

Claudia suggested rather diffidently, "under the circumstances, was that not perhaps the best course of action for him to have taken?"

"But it was horrible!" Evelina wailed. "You don't know. You cannot imagine! The entire day was like a nightmare. I do not know how I possibly got through it. I tried my best to act as though nothing was wrong, but at one point Caroline did ask me if I was feeling quite the thing, and I had to say I had a touch of megrim. But the truth was, there was no way to avoid seeing Rupert make a cake of himself over Mary Whitfield. Can you believe that he attached himself to her all day long, and she flirted with him outrageously?"

For want of words, Claudia clucked again.

"Oh, Aunt, it was ghastly. It was the absolutely worst day of my life."

"I can well imagine."

"No, you cannot," Evelina retorted. "You cannot possibly imagine what it is like to have someone that you were once in love with suddenly turn up to ruin your life all over again." The floods returned full force. "Indeed, you cannot p-possibly know."

"No, of course not." Claudia's voice was wooden. "You are perfectly right. How could I possibly know a thing like that?"

Chapter Eleven

"You appear fagged out, my dear."

Lady Harville was seated by the tea table and looked up at Claudia's entrance.

Of all the lovely rooms in Harville House, the smaller drawing room was Claudia's favorite. Even now it produced a soothing effect with its light blue silk walls and its chairs and sofas covered in rich velvet of the same hue. A darker blue velvet with gold fringe adorned the windows. Their color was repeated in a pair of Derbyshire candelabra and vases placed nearby.

"Do come sit down." The hostess gestured to a chair on the opposite side of the Pembroke table. "Gentlemen may set store by brandy, but I am convinced that tea is quite as rejuvenating without producing those dreadful aftereffects."

Claudia took a restorative sip and smiled her agreement.

"Now, then. Forgive me for meddling, my dear, but I could not fail to overhear the recent storm."

"No. I don't doubt they heard it in Trafalgar Square." Claudia proceeded to explain the cause of Evelina's hysterics.

"Well, well." Lady Harville looked thoughtful as she digested the news. "So Rupert is in London. It appears that Paris did not charm him long."

"No, unfortunately," Claudia sighed.

"Unfortunately? Do you think so? For it is my opinion that he and Evelina will make a perfect match. No, that is doing it too brown. There is no such thing as a perfect match. But I am convinced that they will suit one another very well once they both gain a bit of maturity."

"Oh, but I do not think there is any chance of that. Love's young dream died on the way to Gretna Green."

"Indeed?" Lady Harville's eyes twinkled. "Oh, if only I were the wagering sort, I would have that lovely broach you are wearing before the year is out."

"Surely you mistake the matter. Evelina says he gave her the cold shoulder, as though he had never seen her before in his life."

"Did he indeed? Well, well."

"And flirted outrageously with one of the Miss Whitfields."

"Now I am impressed. Rupert is showing far more sense than I would have credited him with."

"Oh, you are incorrigible." Claudia actually laughed, much to her surprise. The tea, she decided, was indeed having a restorative effect.

"But enough of these halflings." Lady Harville refilled their cups. "Did I not see Thornton escort you home?"

"Why, yes. We happened to see each other at Wedgwood and Byerley's."

Lady Harville's eyebrows shot up. "Indeed?

What a coincidence. Buying a tea set was he?"

"It did seem an unlikely place, I grant you, but there he was. Then he escorted me up Piccadilly to see the czar and grand duchess on parade." Claudia's face grew bleak, and her eyes were fastened on her teacup like a gypsy reading leaves as she gave this edited version of her outing.

The older woman watched her intently. "Well," she said after a lengthy pause, "I observed that he dropped you like a hot chestnut on my doorstep and did not bother to come in."

"Oh dear." Claudia looked embarrassed. "I fear I failed to invite him."

"Never mind. Even had you done so, he would have produced some excuse. He is avoiding me, you see."

"Really?" Claudia dissembled.

"Yes, and for the best of reasons — his freedom. I told you, did I not, that I am matchmaking shamelessly on his behalf?"

"I believe you did mention something of the kind."

"Well, avoiding me will do him no good," the other chuckled. "I have issued a command, posted to his residence. He is to escort you, me, and Lady Frances Kentmere to the theater on Monday night."

"What a formidable array of ladies! Will he agree?"

"Of course he will. He is not so rag-mannered as to refuse his ancient relative."

"And just who is Lady Frances Kentmere?" To her surprise Claudia did not feel quite as disinterested as she tried to sound.

"The perfect match for Thornton, that is who. No beauty, I grant you, but she does quite well enough. She is intelligent and well educated, though not what one would call a bluestocking. Oh, I know he hides the fact well, but Thornton would not be happy with an empty-headed wife. And she is rich as well, though Thornton need not concern himself too much with that. Still, it helps. But best of all, she is Lord Kentmere's daughter. He is one of the leading lights in his majesty's government, you know."

"Are you implying that Lord Thornton has political aspirations? Well, I am amazed."

"Are you? I assure you there is a bit more to Thornton than cards, horses, and light-skirts, though I am not sure even he is aware of it as yet. But they tell me he made a stirring speech in the House against the corn laws some time back. Oh, yes, I think politics will be his forte."

"And thus, Lady Frances." Claudia gave her hostess a speaking look. "You are a regular Machiavelli are you not? I should tremble for my fate should you ever take me on as your project."

"Then, you had best start shaking," the other laughed. "For I have particularly instructed Thornton to provide an escort for you."

Claudia groaned, only partly in jest. The last thing she wished, especially just now, was to be thrown at the head of some stranger. It would be the height of ingratitude, however, to upset her kind hostess's plans. "Could you not have arranged that, too?" was the only protest she allowed herself to utter. "I shudder at the thought of what his lordship may provide."

Lady Harville's eyes were full of mischief, but her voice did not betray it. "I must admit I am curious on that score myself.

"But enough of my matrimonial schemes." She had become quite serious. "I have a far more important matter I wish to discuss with you."

"You have? Why am I suddenly alarmed?"

"No need to be. Except that perhaps you may resent my presumption." She appeared to be feeling her way carefully.

"Yes?" Claudia prodded.

"I have, you see, read your manuscript."

"So soon?"

Claudia, who suffered all the insecurities of an aspiring author, looked apprehensive. It had cost more than she would admit to hand over her creation to Lady Harville. It was like watching a beloved child go off to school, where he would be judged by a whole new set of standards, where affection would have nothing to say in the matter.

She made herself meet Lady Harville's gaze. To her dismay it exhibited an uncharacteristic expression of unease. "You did not care for it," Claudia said bleakly.

The expression underwent a quick sea change, from unease to indignation. "Not care for it? How could I possibly not care for it? You certainly know me well enough by now to appreciate my discernment. Why else would you have trusted me with your story? Not care for it? I loved it. I thought it brilliant. My candle burned all night. I could not put it down till I had discovered its resolution. Not care for it indeed!"

Claudia was weak with relief. "Th-thank you," she managed.

"My heavens, child, you actually looked as though I had driven a stake into your heart. Whatever made you think that I would be disapproving? Surely you must know what good work you have done."

"Not a bit of it. How could one ever know? I collect that all authors must think their creations are special, and of course that isn't true. Besides, you looked so grim."

"Did I? Yes, I see that is possible, for I was seeking the best way to tell you what else I have done."

"Yes?" Claudia was eyeing her hostess anxiously again.

"When you remarked a bit ago that you would hate it if I took you on as a project, well, my dear, I must confess that I have. Not in the romantic realm, rest assured, but in the professional. You see, I have taken the liberty of submitting your manuscript to an acquaintance of mine, a Mr. Edgerton who is in the business of publication."

This time it was merely a teacup and not the teapot that Claudia dropped.

Chapter Twelve

"Whereas it has pleased Almighty God, in His great goodness, to put an end to the long, extended and bloody warfare in which we were engaged against France and her allies, we therefore appoint and command that a General Thanksgiving to Almighty God for these His mercies be observed throughout the United Kingdom called England and Ireland, on Thursday the Seventh Day of July next."

The Regent had issued a proclamation for a special prayer service of Thanksgiving to be held in all places of worship. All loyal subjects were commanded to be present "upon pain of suffering such punishment as may be justly inflicted upon all such as shall condemn or neglect the same."

The threatening tone of the proclamation seemed unnecessary. Loyal subjects were more than willing to give thanks for an end to the long, bloody, and costly war. On the appointed day, St. Paul's was packed with elegantly dressed worshipers eagerly awaiting the dignitaries who were to process into the cathedral.

Lady Harville's party arrived early enough to insure that they were seated well toward the front. Rather to her ladyship's amazement, Lord Thornton had presented himself at Grosvenor Square at what he termed "an ungodly hour" and had offered to escort her and her houseguests.

"How kind. But that will not be necessary. I prefer to save you for more pressing things. The theater, as planned. And I was considering a visit to the opera."

"Oh, God," he groaned. "Well, I'll face that when and if it happens. Right now I intend to save you from being trampled in the crush."

"How gallant." Her tone was dry.

"I rather thought so. You had best set about changing your will in my favor."

"Rogue," she laughed.

He was impeccably groomed for the solemn occasion in a dark blue long-tailed coat and biscuit pantaloons. Even so, Claudia was reminded of their first encounter as they waited together in the entry hall for Evelina to finish dressing and Lady Harville to give last-minute instructions to her cook. "Been shooting the cat, have you?" she inquired pleasantly, looking into his bloodshot eyes.

"No more than usual. Since we had to leave at this ghastly hour, it hardly seemed worthwhile to go to bed."

He appeared determined to rectify this omission, however, for no sooner had he found seats for his charges (placing her ladyship on the aisle for the best possible view with Evelina beside her, leaving Claudia no choice but to sit next to him) than his chin dropped upon his oriental cravat, and he promptly went to sleep. "Ho-hum," his seatmate mused, "having this man asleep beside me is becoming almost commonplace."

She quickly forgot the sleeper, however, when Evelina gasped and clutched her arm with a force that made her jump. "What is wrong?" she whispered.

"I have to leave," Evelina hissed.

"That is impossible," she hissed back.

There was no missing the source of Evelina's distress. Mrs. Whitfield and her daughters were filing into a pew two rows ahead of them accompanied by the Honorable Rupert Hunt.

"She is not going to weep again, is she?" Thornton inquired underneath his breath.

"Oh, do go back to sleep!"

"I cannot bear it!" Evelina was whispering tragically on her other side.

"Pray contain yourself," she whispered back. "Ignore them."

Even she was finding this difficult to do, however, as she watched Rupert bend his head solicitously to attend to some remark from the elder of the Miss Whitfields while their mother gave the young couple an indulgent look.

"Good Lord, he's snared again."

Claudia did not dignify the sleeper's sotto voce observation with a reply. Instead she gazed around for some distraction. Her prayer was answered. A murmur was sweeping through the congregation. "Oh, look, Evelina. That has to be Field Marshal von Blucher."

A white-haired gentleman in Prussian uniform was being escorted to a place of honor. This hero of the battle of Leipzig was the most popular of all the foreign visitors. London had taken him to its heart, and wherever he went he was mobbed by well-wishers. Even Evelina forgot herself long enough to half rise and ogle the celebrity.

Other dignitaries were beginning to arrive, representatives of his majesty's government along with their foreign allies. Claudia steeled herself for the inevitable and was under control when the Grand Duchess of Oldenburg entered with her entourage, which included the handsome, fair-haired Englishman. She was proud of her display of indifference as she studied the magnificent gold plate that adorned the altar. It did little to aid her composure, however, when Thornton roused to crane his neck and stare at the Russian party across the aisle. "Oh, I say," he remarked with cheerful interest, "I do believe the pretty Guardsman is developing a bald spot. Thought you'd like to know."

"I have no idea of whom you are speaking" was the repressive reply.

"Oh well, then." He slumped back down and closed his eyes again, then chuckled under his breath as, despite herself, she turned to look.

"That is the czar's sister." Lady Harville, too, had seen the direction of her gaze and leaned across Evelina to whisper.

"I know. I saw her riding in her carriage the other day."

"Where?" Evelina had come out of her brown study.

"On Piccadilly."

"I mean, where is she now, peagoose."

Claudia pointed out the party, hoping that such intense scrutiny would not alert the target to seek its source. But the blond head (with no evidence of balding) was bent attentively to catch something being whispered into its ear. "He is quite accustomed to being stared at," she thought bitterly.

"I should have expected the grand duchess to be part of the procession," Lady Harville was saying. "The gossipmongers must be right. No ladies are allowed."

The Prince Regent kept the restless congregation waiting for a full hour and a half, leaving it no other occupation than to study what they could see of Sir Christopher Wren's magnificent interior and, of course, to peruse one another. Except for a certain member of the congregation who slept. At one point Claudia felt the necessity, as heads began to turn their way, to dig an elbow in his ribs and cut off the soft snores he was emitting. There was an annoying familiarity to the action. Thornton jerked erect and gave her a baleful stare. At least he did not confuse me with Sophy this time, she thanked her stars.

The dignitaries did at last arrive. It was a noble

procession, led by the lord chancellor and followed by four of the Regent's brothers and his cousin, the Duke of Gloucester, all wearing their trailing ducal robes. His Royal Highness entered next, and a murmur of adulation swept through the crowd. But even Prinny must have been aware that the hero worship was directed, not at him, but at the Duke of Wellington, the great war hero, who marched on his right, carrying the sword of state.

Lady Harville again leaned across Evelina to give Claudia a look that said, Did I not tell you so? And afterward the spectators were to remark to one another disapprovingly that no ladies had been included in the procession. The old queen and her daughters should have been there, they declared, and also the Princess of Wales and Princess Charlotte. But the Regent had decreed otherwise. To include any of the royal ladies would have obliged him to include his detested wife. This he refused to do.

The Thanksgiving service lasted for three hours, with prayers and anthems and a lengthy sermon delivered by the Bishop of Chichester during which Claudia could only envy her companion's ability to sleep. But at last it was all over, and the Regent and his entourage recessed.

The congregation waited courteously for other notables who were not a part of the official procession to leave. Claudia had meant to look anywhere — at the domed ceiling, into the depths of her reticule, anywhere but directly at the recessing celebrities. But her resolution failed. And, like everyone else's, her eyes were upon the grand duchess's party as they passed and had the misfortune to lock with those of the attending Guardsman. His eyes widened; he paled and faltered. For a moment he seemed about to speak, then the forward momentum of his party swept him on.

"Well, that's torn it."

Claudia, fighting for composure, ignored the wide-awake, alert voice at her elbow.

Lady Harville was in the process of suggesting that they wait where they were for the crowd to thin when Evelina pushed past her, practically on the heels of the grand duchess's party, muttering something about wishing to see the royals leave. In truth, she had decided that if she were forced to sit another minute watching Rupert Hunt be the willing target of that simpering widgeon Miss Whitfield, she would scream St. Paul's down.

"Evelina, wait!" Claudia's command fell upon deaf ears. "Oh, we will never find her in this crush," she moaned.

"Damnation!" Thornton offered.

"Pray remember where you are," Claudia snapped.

"Come on. Let's try and follow the little peagoose." He took both ladies firmly by their arms and began to force their way up the clogged aisle.

At least the Russians have had time to get away, Claudia thought thankfully as they attempted to hold a position at the top of the steps and scan the crowd below for a pink gros de Naples bonnet. The Regent had been the first to leave, hurrying away in his yellow carriage. To her relief Claudia spied the grand duchess and her escort in a stylish barouche not far behind.

"There she is!"

For a moment Claudia thought Thornton was referring to the Russian duchess, so distracted from her mission had she become.

"You two stay together while I go fetch Niobe," he barked as he hurried off, parting a path for himself with little consideration of the consequences. Lady Harville took advantage of the driven wedge and pulled Claudia along with her in his wake.

Evelina had not been as fortunate in her progression. She came to regret her impulsive dash, for she was soon propelled by the rush of folk leaving St. Paul's into the crush waiting outside the church and swept along in pursuit of the yellow carriage. Her reticule was ripped from her grasp immediately. This was just as well, for she needed both hands free to maintain her balance as she was jostled first against one running figure and then another. She stumbled and knew she was fated to be trampled under foot but was far too spent to scream. At that moment she was snatched up by a pair of strong arms and thrown like a bag of grain across a broad dark blue shoulder.

Lord Thornton used his free arm to part the

crowd and force his way back to the steps of St. Paul's, where Lady Harville and Claudia were waiting anxiously.

"She's not hurt, just scared," he reassured them while he lowered the sobbing girl from his shoulder. He retained a protective arm around her and a resigned expression while she wept copiously onto his shoulder, soaking the superfine.

"Thank you. I can never express —" Claudia had begun when a cyclone erupted suddenly in their midst. Young Rupert Hunt, his face contorted with fury, jerked Evelina out of his brother's arms. "Let go of her, you lecher!" he said between clinched teeth while at the same time landing a bruising facer on his lordship's jaw.

"And as for you," he turned to glare at his erstwhile fiancée, "no need to set your cap for him. I can tell you right now he's nothing but a here-and-therein where females are concerned."

The Honorable Rupert wheeled and left as abruptly as he had come, while his astonished brother stared after him, rubbing his damaged jaw, trying to decide whether to murder or commit him.

All the drama of the day had been too much for Claudia. She gave in to an onslaught of uncontrollable laughter. "Your brother clearly is a splendid judge of character," she finally managed to gasp. "I only wish that Edwin could have been here to see you get your own back."

Lord Thornton continued to massage his jaw while he glared in her direction.

Chapter Thirteen

"I should never have dreamed that Lord Thornton has a *tendre* for me."

Claudia's jaw dropped. The book she was holding almost followed suit. She might just as well have dropped it. Evelina had put a period to her reading.

When her niece had invaded the bedchamber some ten minutes earlier, Claudia had supposed she wished to talk. But Evelina had seemed content to wander about the room, examining this paperweight and that picture, the view from the window, the flowers in the bedside vase. Claudia's nerves were already frayed from all the shocks they had endured the day before. She had barely resisted the urge to snap, "Oh, for pity's sake, Evelina, do sit down!" when her niece did so and uttered her preposterous statement.

Claudia took a moment to recover. "Lord Thornton a *tendre* for you? I think perhaps that you mistake the matter."

"Oh?" Evelina bristled and drew herself upright in the painted armchair, where initially she had displayed a deplorable tendency to slouch. "And why should he not have?"

"Well, the obvious answer is that you are much, much too young for him."

"Pooh!" Evelina waved that objection away.

"My age has nothing to say in the matter. Gentlemen are always choosing much younger females for their wives. Take Sir Geoffrey back home, for example. Why the second Lady Lawrence is actually younger than his eldest son."

Claudia had no ready answer for this observation.

The conversation languished for a moment with both ladies boggled in their thoughts. Evelina resumed it. "Am I pretty?" she blurted.

"You do well enough." Her aunt's tone was repressive.

"Well enough?" Evelina wrinkled her nose. "Rupert once told me that I was a diamond of the first water."

"He perhaps lacked objectivity."

"Oh, I do hope you are not about to read me a lecture upon vanity and come up with some platitude about character and conduct being of far more importance than one's looks, for I'll not believe it. At least I won't as far as gentlemen are concerned."

Claudia, who was about to do just that, coughed instead. "I do fear you have a point," she conceded.

"Then, pray give me a straight answer. Am I pretty?"

"Well, then, yes. I do believe that most people would consider you so. And when you are a bit older —"

Evelina waved the future away. "I am not concerned with years from now. What I really wish to know is am I as pretty as Mary Whitfield?"

"You surely cannot expect me to be a judge of that. I am inclined to be prejudiced, you know."

"Oh, for heaven's sake, Claudia! I might just as well be talking to Papa."

"I'm sorry. I confess I am trying to think what he might say. But in all objectivity, yes, you are much prettier than Miss Whitfield."

"Thank you. I thought as much. But she is far more flirtatious than I am. And I do think that gentlemen respond to flattery as least as much as they do to beauty. Perhaps even more so."

"Oh, I quite agree." The corners of Claudia's mouth were inclined to twitch, but she answered gravely. "I am curious, though. Does it matter to you how Rupert feels about her?"

"N-no. Of course not. It is just that I find it puzzling that he should attack his brother in that manner."

"Yes, I, too, wondered about that."

"Pray tell me, just what is a lecher?"

"Er, well, the term refers to a man who is overly fond of women — in a certain way."

"Seduces a lot of them, you mean?"

"I collect that would be one definition."

"And do you think that Lord Thornton is one of those? Lechers, I mean."

"I really could not say."

"Well, Rupert should know. Men generally do."

Claudia, feeling that the conversational waters were rising above her head, looked pointedly at the mantel clock.

"Should we not dress for dinner?" she suggested.

Lord Thornton was dressing for the theater. His valet, having discarded two abortive attempts to reach perfection, stood back to survey the mathematical arrangement of the heavily starched and pristine cravat with satisfaction. His lordship's slightly bored reflection in the glass turned to hostility as his brother's image appeared suddenly above his shoulder. Unlike his lordship, Rupert was not in evening clothes but wore a dapper-looking gray tailcoat, fawn pantaloons, and black boots.

"If you have come to apologize, pray be quick about it, for as you can see, I am going out. But if you desire another dustup, I can always delay my departure a bit.

"That will do, Lindsey." Thornton dismissed the valet who was gazing back and forth at the brothers with some alarm.

As the door closed behind the servant, Rupert looked at his brother's bruised jaw with satisfaction.

"Got you a good 'un, didn't I?"

"Oh, yes indeed." Thornton touched his face gingerly. "And I'll tell you right now if you had loosened a tooth, it would be bellows to mend for you. Now, why are you here, whelp? You would have been well-advised to put considerable time and distance between us after yesterday's little contretemps. I have been debating between sending you off to rusticate and thrashing you within an inch of your life."

"Oh? And do you think you can do either?" Hackles were rising.

"Yes. And you damn well know it. Now, why are you here?"

"Well, I had meant to beg pardon for catching you unawares, but I no longer feel inclined to do so."

"Good evening, then."

"Not quite so fast. My main reason for coming is to tell you to keep your hands off Miss Wentworth."

"Indeed?" His lordship was looking decidedly dangerous. "And to which Miss Wentworth do you refer?"

"Evelina, and you dashed well know it. She was the one you were publicly pawing in that disgusting fashion. And from now on, I am warning you, keep your hands off her."

The older brother gave the younger a level look. "Very well, then, if you insist. I shall certainly bear that in mind the next time the little cawker is on the verge of being trampled by a mob."

"W-what?"

"You heard me right. Young Miss Wentworth had rushed into the thick of the crowd following Prinny's carriage and got knocked off her feet. I saw no other way to extricate her from that predicament without a hands-on approach."

"Oh."

"Yes, 'oh.' And furthermore, let it be understood between us that my lechery does not extend toward the infantry."

"Oh," his brother repeated, turning red. "I did call you a lecher, didn't I."

"Yes, you did. At the top of your lungs and within hearing of three-quarters of the ton."

"Oh, well, then," the other gulped. "I really should beg your pardon."

"Yes, you should. But frankly I haven't the time let alone the inclination to listen. The process would bore me to tears. So off with you, halfling."

"I'm no halfling," Rupert growled as he turned toward the door.

"I stand corrected but damned if I will beg your pardon, either. Just one minute, though." He stopped his brother's hand from turning the doorknob. "I must confess that my curiosity has the better of me. Could you please explain why you felt obliged to play knight-errant to my evil ogre in Miss Evelina's defense? Don't tell me you still have romantic feelings toward her."

"No, of course not. I thank the Lord daily for my narrow escape. It is just that —"

"Yes?" his brother prodded as Rupert's voice trailed off.

"It is just that once a cove has actually eloped with a particular female, he feels rather responsible for her, don't you know."

"No, actually I don't. But I defer to your superior wisdom in this case."

Chapter Fourteen

Lady Harville had invited the theatergoers to dine. "In order for you young folk to become acquainted," she explained to Claudia. "The performance rules out conversation. At least it should," she amended.

For her part, Claudia had small hope and even less desire to form friendships with this particular party. So she was surprised, or perhaps disappointed, when she took an immediate liking to Lady Frances Kentmere, who was first to arrive at Grosvenor Square. As far as it went, Lady Harville's description had been accurate. Lady Frances was not a pretty woman, but she had a neat figure, a pleasant countenance, and fine gray eyes that revealed humor and intelligence. As usual, Claudia concluded after a lively discussion of the foreign visitors and their political jockeying, Lady Harville had not erred in her judgment. Lady Frances would make Thornton the perfect wife.

The hostess was just beginning to glance at her longcase clock when the gentlemen were announced. "How rag-mannered of you, Thornton," she said severely as two Bond Street beaus in black and white evening dress strode into the drawing room.

"Blame my friend, here," the other responded

cheerfully as he bent over his aunt's hand. "Couldn't get his cravat right. And I refused to be seen with him till he did. Ought to dismiss that cowhand valet if you ask me, old fellow."

"I didn't ask you. And Charles does very well, thank you, when he doesn't have a high-stickler like you looking down the nose at him."

"Well, you both look splendid," her ladyship interposed. "Thornton, present your friend to the ladies — no, no need to include me. Mr. Stanesby was a mere lad at Eton when I met him. But he made a lasting impression, I assure you. And no need to look alarmed, sir, I have no intention of betraying the reason why."

Everyone laughed as the gentlemen turned the ladies' way. But in Claudia's case, amusement changed to shock. She had thought the round-faced young man with his slightly protruding eyes and thinning fair hair looked vaguely familiar but had attributed it to type. Then, as he focused his beaming smile on her, it was all she could manage not to gasp. He was one of the cardplayers she had interrupted at Hunter's Hall.

"Miss Wentworth, may I present Mr. Stanesby," his lordship was saying. Claudia was too occupied with maintaining her composure to notice the mischievous look in Thornton's eyes.

Mr. Stanesby appeared puzzled as he acknowledged the introduction. "Have we not met before, Miss Wentworth? What I mean to say is, you somehow look familiar."

Thornton, standing slightly behind his friend, elected to look thunderstruck, which did little to help calm Claudia's nerves.

"I think not, Mr. Stanesby," she managed to answer. "This is my first visit to London, you see."

Lord Thornton appeared to recover rapidly. He shot her a look of abject apology over his friend's shoulder. "What a ramshackle thing to say, Linley. Once met, Miss Wentworth could not possibly be forgot. By the by, Miss Wentworth, may I say you are looking quite the thing this evening?" His quizzing glass appraised her evening dress of Urling's net over pale blue satin with approval. It lingered longest upon her hair, dressed in the French style with a few curls framing the face and the rest piled high upon the crown of her head and encircled by a garland of roses.

"You are right, of course," Mr. Stanesby smiled, but he still looked bemused as he turned to smile at Lady Frances.

"May I have a word with you, Aunt?" Thornton whispered as the others chatted. He pulled her aside and murmured in her ear a moment. She looked aghast, and then annoyed. But when the butler appeared upon the threshold seconds later, she organized her group with resignation.

"Mr. Stanesby, if you will take Lady Frances in to dinner, my nephew will contrive to escort both Miss Wentworth and myself."

The arrangement held throughout the evening. Claudia managed a private word with her escort as they entered Covent Garden behind the others.

"Is this your idea of a joke?" she fumed.

"I am sure I don't know what you mean." His face was all innocence, but his eyes danced with mischief.

"And I am sure you do. I doubt you are overly blessed with friends, but I cannot believe that you were so desperate as to be compelled to show up with one of that drunken group who were playing cards with you on that ghastly night. I can only assume that you will enjoy seeing my character left in shreds."

"There is not the slightest danger of that, I assure you. Linley was far too deep in his cups to recall the incident."

"Indeed? You heard him. He is certain we have met. He will eventually put two and two together."

"Not a chance of it. Linley hasn't the intellect to add two and two. And he was thoroughly disguised the night that you abducted me. As you should know."

"What I know is you should not have brought him. It was pure mischief on your part, if not sadism. And you are enjoying my discomfort. Do not deny it."

"Oh, but I do deny it. What I am really enjoying is upsetting my aunt's little schemes. You see, after I had explained your and Linley's — err — past history, she had no choice but to throw

Lady Frances at his head instead of mine. Couldn't risk jogging the old boy's memory, don't you see. And look —" He nodded toward Lady Frances and Mr. Stanesby, who stood in animated conversation while Lady Harville chatted with an acquaintance. "They are getting along famously, you see." He grinned wickedly.

Thornton ushered the party into his box, placing the ladies in the best vantage point to see the stage with the gentlemen in easy conversational range behind them. Claudia was too engrossed by her surroundings to take part in the small talk of her more sophisticated companions.

Their box was situated two tiers up above the apron of the stage. "You are well placed" — Thornton bent forward to inform her as she leaned upon the railing to look down below — "to spit upon Mr. Sinclair's head if you dislike his portrayal of Richard the Lion Heart."

"Isn't it time for one of your famous naps?" she replied, not turning around.

"Oh, no," he answered cheerfully. "I usually save that for the second act."

She leaned farther forward, gloved elbows resting on the ledge, drinking in the magnificence of the theater, uncaring whether such naive pleasure marked her as a flat from out of town. For her it was a fairyland. The stage was hung with crimson curtains. A drop scene represented a temple dedicated to William Shakespeare. Three circles of boxes, with crimson hangings and light blue seat covers, ringed the gallery. The entire theater was ablaze with hundreds of candles that illuminated the splendor of an audience adorned in their finest. Diamonds glittered; ostrich feathers, animated by the movements of elegantly coiffed heads, waved. The ladies were a kaleidoscope of every color. The gentlemen were starkly elegant in black and white with here and there a scarlet uniform to break the masculine monotony. Claudia's perusal passed over, returned, and froze upon one particular uniform. She quickly slid back from her exposed position into the recesses of their box. She snapped open her ivory fan and plied it rapidly across her face.

"Warm are you?" the annoying voice murmured. "And here I was wondering if you might possibly need a cloak."

"Are you all right, my dear?" Lady Harville turned away from Lady Frances to inquire solicitously.

"Oh, yes. Perfectly. A bit giddy, perhaps, from gazing down. And from the excitement. That is all. It is quite magnificent, is it not?" She managed a weak smile.

"Yes, indeed. One forgets, I fear, what a first impression the Theatre Royal can make."

"Not to mention the notables in the audience." The annoying murmur was back again. "I do believe our ubiquitous Guardsman is gazing this way again. Fan up, Miss Wentworth."

Involuntarily the ivory flew to conceal her

face. She forced it down again as Thornton chuckled.

Claudia sat up straighter, folded her hands in her lap, and stared rigidly at the still-empty stage. She would not, she would *not* allow the fact that he was seated only yards away, directly across the boards of the stage, spoil the evening for her. What was done was done. He belonged to a long-distant, long-dead past. She was a mature woman now. Twenty-seven years old, for heaven's sake. Such flutterings and palpitations belonged to her salad days. They were leftovers from when she was a green, naive girl; reflex actions brought on by the unwelcome resurrection of memories long buried and totally inappropriate now. Dimly she grew aware of a gradual hush. The conductor was raising his arms. A swell of music filled the auditorium. Thank God, the performance had begun.

At the interval, Lady Harville excused herself to go visit a neighboring box. Mr. Stanesby suggested that the rest of them stroll in the corridor. "Legs need stretching, you know." Claudia begged off, claiming that she was far too interested in the audience milling below her to leave her vantage point.

"You two go on. I prefer to continue my nap right here," Thornton told his friend, much to Claudia's annoyance. During the performance he had been sprawled in his chair, his long legs stretched between the seats in front of him. But as soon as the other two had left the box, he moved up to sit beside her. "Don't let me keep you here," she smiled frostily. "A bit of exercise might help keep you awake."

"A state to be avoided at all costs," he answered cheerfully. "But tell me, are we waiting or simply skulking here?"

"As usual, I've no idea what you mean."

"Haven't you?" He was staring across the stage at a movement in the opposite box. "Well, never mind. I have my answer. Shall we at least stand?"

"If you wish." She rose, deploring the sudden weakness in her knees.

"There, that is better. Now, move back from the edge. Mustn't risk giddiness, you know." He had a firm grasp on her arm and guided her to the side of the box, partially hid from view. "Ah, this is better," he murmured. "Definitely a tactical advantage. I do think I hear footsteps coming our way, don't you?"

"I have heard nothing but footsteps," she snapped. Most of the audience seemed to be promenading back and forth outside their box.

"But it is a particular pair of footsteps that I hear. Ah, yes. What did I tell you?"

Just as the box curtains parted, Thornton pulled her close and bent his head. His lips tenderly brushed hers. The Guardsman on the threshold turned to stone.

Chapter Fifteen

Claudia leapt backward out of Thornton's arms, elbowing him sharply as she did so. Her face was a flaming red.

"Looking for someone?" his lordship inquired affably.

The Guardsman's recovery was quick. "As a matter of fact, I am." He smiled charmingly at Claudia. His voice was husky. "I could not really believe my eyes at first. I was sure I must be dreaming. But it is really you."

"Changed a bit, has she?" Thornton inquired with interest.

"No. That is, yes. She is even more beautiful than I remember."

"I say. Are you quite sure you have the right lady? Miss Wentworth here is a rather common type. Chances are —"

"What an unexpected pleasure to see you again, Hugo."

Claudia credited her remarkable composure to the fact that her deep desire to murder Lord Thornton had taken precedence over her earlier palpitations at the sight of her long-lost love. "I had no idea that you were in London."

"That's odd. I could have sworn —" Thornton had begun when she interrupted. "Oh, may I present you to Lord Thornton? Captain Landseer is an old, old friend of mine."

Thornton was squinting at the other's insignia. "I don't claim to be an expert on military matters, but surely it is *Major* Landseer, is it not?"

"Yes, as a matter of fact." The smile at Claudia could have melted the most resisting heart. "I have been promoted since last we met."

"That wouldn't be the only change in your status, would it?" Thornton offered helpfully. "Married now, ain't you, if I am not mistaken?"

The major wrested his eyes from Claudia's face to look at her companion. The look was not a cordial one. "I am sorry to have to ask, but do we know one another? I fear I cannot recall."

"Oh, no, no. We have never actually met. But you are something of a celebrity you know — hithering and thithering with the czar and the grand duchess. And we do have a mutual friend, I collect. Colonel McKinney." He beamed at the newcomer, apparently delighted to have established a common ground.

"I see." There was a decided lack of enthusiasm in the major's voice.

"Couldn't help but notice the similarity of uniform. Mentioned it to McKinney. He told me you had married into the Russian family, so to speak. Have a child or two, don't you, as best I recall."

"That is correct," the other answered repressively just as the box curtain opened and Lady Frances and Mr. Stanesby returned.

How many times during the intervening years had she imagined meeting Hugo Landseer again? Claudia wondered. But never in her wildest dreams was the meeting so absurd, so bogged down in introductions.

"May I present Major Landseer, an old friend of mine? Major Landseer, Lady Frances Kentmere and Mr. Stanesby."

The introductions were acknowledged graciously. "Known each other long have you?" Mr. Stanesby asked.

"Oh, yes. Donkey's years." Lord Thornton helpfully supplied.

The major appeared to have decided that the best tactic with his lordship was to ignore him. "Miss Wentworth and I have been acquainted all our lives. My father was vicar of Mansfield."

"A clergyman's son, are you?" Thornton digested this bit of news. "I see. That probably explains your warlike bent."

Mr. Stanesby also seemed struck by the major's revelation. "You are from Mansfield?" The question was for Claudia. "I was there myself not long ago. Thornton has a country house near there. But then, I expect you know that."

"Why, yes, it is common knowledge in the village that Hunter's Hall belongs to his lordship."

"So that is who you are." The major's eyes did not echo the polite smile he directed toward Lord Thornton. "As I recall, the place was seldom, if ever, used when I was growing up."

"True. My father disliked leaving the Metropolis. But I have since discovered that the area does have a certain charm."

"Oh, yes indeed. Seemed like a very pleasant sort of place," Mr. Stanesby chimed in. "Not that we saw all that much of it. Actually, we played cards most of the time," he explained to Lady Frances. "Went up there to shoot, but somehow never actually got around to it. You know how it is."

"No, I really cannot say that I do," she laughed up at him.

"Pity, though. I had no idea you were in the neighborhood, Miss Wentworth," he continued gallantly. "Would have been certain to call. Not that I knew you then of course. Thornton here should have made a point of getting to know his neighbors. Shabby of him not to. As it was, we never met a soul —" His voice trailed off a bit, and he looked at Claudia oddly. At this moment Lady Harville joined them. To Claudia's relief, Mr. Stanesby seemed to dismiss whatever idea he was entertaining.

This time Thornton did the polite and presented the major to her ladyship. The two of them chatted amiably for a few moments, discovering mutual acquaintances, then the Guardsman excused himself to return to his box. "It has been a pleasure to see you again, Miss Wentworth," he said as he left. The words were formal. But the eyes conveyed a wealth of things left unsaid. The episode had left Claudia feeling drained and shaky. She sat down gratefully.

"What an extraordinarily handsome young man," Lady Harville was remarking.

"Oh, yes," Thornton agreed with an enthusiasm that Claudia realized was meant to irritate her. It succeeded. "Quite dazzling, in fact. And charming, too. Let us not forget charming."

The performance began again. Later, when Lady Harville spoke complimentarily about the quality of the acting, Claudia would agree wholeheartedly. But the truth was she could recall nothing of what took place upon the stage.

No, that was not quite accurate. There had been a moment in Act III during a "Dance Incidental to the Piece" when the intensity in Mr. Stanesby's voice as he whispered to Lord Thornton snapped her from her reverie. "I say, ain't that — you know? The second girl from the left, I mean. Of that bunch in the back row."

Claudia did focus her attention then upon the stage, where a dozen opera dancers in diaphanous costumes reaching barely below their knees were leaping gracefully about. In aid of what, she had no idea.

"Yes, it is." The growl in Thornton's low reply was obviously meant to be repressive. Claudia looked curiously at "the bunch in the back" now propelled downstage by the requirements of the dance.

"She is certainly a stunner." Stanesby's voice was awed. "You lucky dog!"

Claudia stared harder. It was difficult to distinguish features at their distance, but the figure of the second girl, revealingly displayed, was voluptuous enough to stun any male. The golden curls enhanced the general effect, and her movements were clearly seductive. More so, Claudia thought censoriously, than was strictly called for.

She was almost certain that this was Sophy. She tried to remember the names printed upon the playbill. Impossible. And even if she could have done, the information would not have helped. Christian names were never used. And most female performers were billed as Mrs. So and So, usually more as a courtesy than a reflection of the female's actual status.

The interminable performance finally crept to its close. How ironic, Claudia mused, that what should have been the evening of her dreams had taken on such a nightmarish quality. But at least, she thanked her stars as they stood waiting outside the theater for their carriage to inch its way up the thronged street, she did not see the grand duchess's party anywhere. She did not believe she could endure another encounter with Hugo. Immediately on the heels of this thought a "hssst!" sounded behind her. When she turned, a lad wearing a livery she did not recognize pressed something into her hand, then melted back into the crowd.

It had all happened very quickly. But not quickly enough, she realized as she surreptitiously slipped the card into her reticule. Lord Thornton was watching the maneuver with a half smile on his face.

"Doesn't believe in letting the grass grow under his feet much, does he?" he remarked.

Chapter Sixteen

Claudia crossed Grosvenor Square green in a daze, still at odds with her better judgment.

Initially it had been in the driver's seat. She had reached her bedchamber the night before, undressed with the assistance of her abigail, and had climbed into her four-poster before looking at the message that had been slipped surreptitiously to her. On the back of Hugo's engraved calling card was scrawled in pencil "Must see you. The royal library. Bond Street. Tomorrow. Eleven o'clock."

Her first reaction had been indignation. Does he think I will come running at his summons after all that has happened? She flung the card in the direction of the fireplace. The force of her emotion would have propelled a more solid object across the room. But the piece of cardboard merely fluttered to the floor beside her bed, where, after a near-sleepless night, she retrieved it next morning before the maid could do so.

And in the cold light of day, it had seemed reasonable to meet with Hugo. After all, she did have books to return. And if he needed to clear his conscience, an impossible feat as far as she was concerned, why begrudge him the effort? Perhaps it would serve her, too, as an exorcism.

After all these years she could finally write "finis" to a phase of her life that she should have had done with long ago.

Or maybe not, she thought as she walked across the green, arms loaded with books, head down, her resolution wavering. The mere sight of Hugo had been enough to upset a hard-fought-for equilibrium. God alone knew what a tête-à-tête might do. Throw her back to the state of mind (or *mindlessness* might be a more apt description of being in love) that she had been in nine years before? To be obliged to live through all that heartache again? It was unthinkable. She was a fool to risk it. Nonetheless she could not turn back.

"Ahem." A throat cleared stagily. Lord Thornton stood a few feet away, blocking her path.

The sight of him, removing his beaver, bowing with a smile on his face that she construed as mocking, was like a crimson cloth waved before an agitated bull.

"What are you doing here?" she demanded. "How dare you follow me!"

His brows shot up. "Follow you? Forgive my saying so, but someone with a bit more acumen might have noted that I am headed in quite the opposite direction. But then, I should not judge you too harshly, I collect. Your mind is obviously upon your assignation." He gestured toward the books. "In the library, I see. How thoughtful of the major. You can meet quite by chance. Very respectable, albeit cloth-headed on your part.

But then, who am I to judge" — he reached inside his coat to pull out a folded note and wave it before her — "since I, too, have an assignation."

"Indeed? With Sophy, I have no doubt. Is she perhaps an opera dancer? I marvel she can write."

His eyebrows did their acrobatic thing again. "That, Miss Wentworth, is a most improper question coupled with a very cattish observation."

"You are right." She had the grace to look embarrassed. It did not last. "But you are certainly in no position to preach propriety to me. Your behavior last night could hardly have been more improper."

"Oh, you think not?" He grinned down at her. "You don't know the world as well as you think if you believe that. But I would like to —" He was suddenly at a loss for words.

"Apologize? That really is not necessary." She made a move to pass him, but he took her firmly by the arm.

"You are damned right, it isn't necessary. Nor do I intend to apologize. I will explain my behavior, however, since the point of it seems to have escaped you."

"I have no need of any explanations, I assure you." When she attempted to jerk away, her books tumbled from her arms. He stooped and picked them up.

"I've no desire to carry your curst books, but I

will take them as far as that." He nodded to a cast-iron bench underneath a shade tree.

"I do not intend —" she began, but he was already striding off with the library's property. She reluctantly moved out of the way of a nursemaid with two toddlers on leading strings, and followed.

"I do not intend to engage in a coze with you," she continued. "Now, if you will give me those books." He had seated himself upon the bench, still holding them upon his knee.

"Oh, for God's sake, sit down!" he snapped. "Make the tin soldier wait for a few minutes. Where is your pride, Miss Wentworth?"

"How dare you speak to me like that! And what does pride have to say to anything? I am going to meet an old friend, that is all. I see no reason for your insinuations."

"The devil you don't! Sit!" He reached out for her hand and pulled her down beside him. She retrieved the hand but made no move to rise.

"There, that is better. I am about to reverse our usual roles, you see, and ring a peal over you for a change. For, I must say, I am very disappointed in you, Claudia."

"There is no need, I am certain, to ask in what way."

"Not the slightest need. For I intend to tell you."

"I thought as much."

"You see, I have always considered you a woman of unusual common sense."

"Why do I suspect that is not a compliment?"

"For the same reason you suspect every word I say, I would suppose. But let's not get off the subject. As I was saying, from the moment we first met, I was impressed with the way you were able to keep your head and hold your ground in a very awkward situation."

"Awkward? That seems a namby-pamby term for breaking up a drunken card game in a debauched bachelor establishment in the middle of the night."

"So my vocabulary is not as extensive as yours. Though I needs must point out that you use the term 'debauched' rather loosely. But quit trying to change the subject."

"We have no subject." She started to rise. "And I must —"

He prevented the maneuver by re-gripping her arm and holding her there. "Let him wait!" he said between clinched teeth. "After what he has done, all he has to do is whistle, and you still come running? As I was saying, I am very disappointed in you, Claudia. The fellow jilted you, for God's sake!"

She turned pale, tried to speak, and couldn't.

"Oh, dear God. I am sorry. That was unforgivable. I should have phrased that better. It's my limited vocabulary again."

"Not at all," she rallied. " 'Jilted' is the mot juste. But tell me. How did you come to know that? It all happened aeons ago. I have not confided even in Lady Harville. And I hardly think my broken betrothal would have been the *on dit* of London drawing rooms."

"Rupert told me that you once had plans to marry."

"Rupert!"

"What is so strange about that? My brother and your niece spent many hours together before hatching their rattle-brained scheme of haring off to Gretna Green. I doubt that either of our families has any skeletons left hidden in our closets."

"So that is what my betrothal was," she bristled, "a skeleton in the closet?"

"Not really. For your niece believes your lover died heroically in the war. She sees you as a tragic heroine. I learned your major's history from a military friend. That he had —"

"*Jilted* me?"

"Cried off for a fortune. What I fail to understand is why, instead of dancing a jig in sheer relief, you allowed his infidelity to ruin your life."

"I did no such thing!"

"I beg to differ. Here you are, a beautiful, desirable woman of a certain age, who has not had a single suitor since Prince Charming did his disappearing act."

"How like a man to think that simply because I wished to have no further dealings with your sex, my life was ruined. I can assure you that is far from the case. I have been most fulfilled."

"Playing nursemaid to your weepy niece? I'll not believe it."

"What you choose to believe is your own affair. And to speak plainly, I fail to see why you should concern yourself with mine."

"Yes, that is a poser," he answered thoughtfully. "I collect it must have to do with the fact that when you've foiled an elopement with a person, you feel a certain obligation to her."

She stared at him blankly. "That makes no sense whatever."

"You are right," he sighed, "it doesn't. Seemed to when Rupert said something to that effect. But, I forget that the circumstances are not quite the same. Perhaps it is best just to repeat that I do admire you."

"Oh, yes," her voice was filled with scorn, "you have made that quite evident."

"It happens to be true. That is why I am anxious for you to wake up to the fact that your long-lost love is a scoundrel."

"You have no basis for that slander. You do not even know him."

"Oh, the opinion is widely held, believe me. I cannot understand why a woman of sense like yourself doesn't see it. Of course you were a mere child with more hair than wit when you succumbed to his charms. And I am sure you have exaggerated your grand passion ever since. And made excuses for his betrayal." He felt her stiffen. "Struck a nerve there, did I? And he certainly is pretty. I will concede him that much."

There was a hostile pause. "Have you quite finished? May I go now?"

"No. I have not said what I had intended."

"I can assure you that you have said quite enough."

"Not true. I have not yet explained last night's behavior."

"I do not wish to hear it."

"I acted in that — well — lover-like fashion for your sake."

"How gallant!"

"No need to take that tone. It was rather. Should it not gall you a bit for the soldier to discover that after he threw you over for a fortune and went on to father one and three-quarters children that all you have done is pine?"

"That is not so!"

"No? Well, if it appears so to me, it is bound to give the same impression to that puffed-up jackanapes. So I wished to give him something to think about. He should not take you so for granted."

"You are too, too kind." In case he did not catch the sarcasm, she added with a withering glare, "Now, if I may, I have these books to return." Once more she started to rise. The nursemaid and her charges, retracing their steps, looked on with interest.

"Very well," he sighed. "It seems I have made no impression at all. Oh, what the devil! One last throw then."

He pulled her back down into his arms, and when she raised her startled face, he impatiently pushed her bonnet back to dangle from its ribbons and placed his lips roughly upon hers that were just beginning to part in protest. The kiss was lengthy and very, very expert. It left Claudia draped against his chest and the toddlers staring with their fingers in their mouths.

"I must go now."

She at last managed to extricate herself, rise, and begin to walk away.

"Wait!" He started after her. "Don't forget your books."

"Oh."

She turned, and he placed the volumes in her arms.

"Enjoy your tête-à-tête," he said dryly. "At least you can now tell your hero that you have been made love to since he left you and England in the lurch."

Chapter Seventeen

"You damned fool!"

The Viscount Thornton was furious. He kicked a stone from his path as he walked reluctantly toward Lady Harville's town house cursing himself for ten varieties of an idiot. What had come over him to lose his head in such a fashion? To treat the self-possessed and haughty Miss Wentworth like some doxy of an upstairs maid? It was unthinkable. Impulsive. And totally out of character. In the past his follies, and God knows they were legion, had been entered into with his eyes wide open.

He looked grim as he clanged the iron door knocker. He was now adding the folly of responding to Evelina's request for an interview to his list of sins. If he considered the business objectively, and, by George, it was high time that he did, his motive had more to do with the chance of seeing the aunt than with talking to the niece. Well, he had seen Claudia Wentworth all right. And a proper dog's dinner he had made of that.

Lady Harville's butler greeted him warmly but regretted that his mistress was not at home. Over the major domo's shoulder, Thornton saw Evelina descending the staircase. She was wearing a white muslin morning dress with a pink ribbon encircling the empire waistline, and for once her features seemed composed. She did, in fact, look young and fresh and fetching, and it was not difficult for Thornton to see how she could easily have turned his brother's head. My God, I *am* turning into a lecher, was his disgusted thought.

His face and voice revealed none of this turmoil, however, as he handed the butler his hat and stepped inside. "Never mind. I'll come in anyway and visit a moment with Miss Evelina."

She ordered tea served in the small drawing room. Her hand, he noted, was not quite steady as she filled his cup from a heavy, ornate silver teapot. She was unused to playing hostess, of course. He trusted that was the cause of her nervousness and not his proximity.

He endured her stabs at conversation — the likelihood of rain, the crowded London streets — for a much longer period than his patience had lasted. But at length he was goaded into saying, gently, he trusted, "I believe you had some purpose in inviting me here, Miss Wentworth."

"Yes, I did." She put down her cup but continued to stare at it. "It is difficult, you see, to know how to go about it."

"I find that the best way usually is to simply be direct."

She shot him a glance then. "Yes, you would think that of course."

Ouch. There was a bit of her aunt in young Miss Wentworth.

"The thing is, I feel I should try and make amends. I am mortified —" She paused. "Well, heartsick, actually, would be more exact."

"Oh, please, please spare me any more theatrics," he pleaded, but, with effort, silently.

"You see, it is a terrible thing, Lord Thornton, to have been the cause of a quarrel between two brothers."

"Oh, well, then. If you mean Rupert and me, you should not refine too much upon it. It was nothing really."

"Nothing! You call it nothing when he flew at you like a — a —"

"Maniac?" he supplied. This seemed a difficult day for everyone's vocabulary.

"I should have said more like an avenging fury," she corrected starchily, proving his point. "I had never seen Rupert so enraged. I would not have imagined that he could attack you like that."

"Nor I." The other winced and touched his cheek gingerly where a faint bruise still remained. "Had I done, I would have at least ducked."

"At any rate, please accept my heartfelt apology."

"If you wish, I will do so. But as I said, you should not refine too much upon the incident. It is quite common for brothers to be at daggers drawn. Goes all the way back to Cain and Abel, I expect. No, that's coming it a bit too strong. I doubt that Rupert had murder in his heart. The point is, Miss Wentworth, that the only amazing thing is that we had never before that come to blows. Well, *blow* to be more exact." It still rankled that he had been caught off guard. "Our great difference in age kept us peaceable, I collect, so forget the incident is my advice."

"It was not only what Rupert did that was so terrible," she persisted. "It was also what he said." She grew a bit pink. "He called you a most terrible name, if you recall."

"Yes, as a matter of fact, I do."

"It was most mistaken of him. In this instance, at any rate."

"Why, thank you," he said dryly.

She was too preoccupied to pick up any nuances of tone. "I feel it my duty, you see, to set things right between you. And so —" She was fumbling in her bosom. While he watched in fascination, she extracted a folded piece of paper. "I have written him a note."

"Good Lord," Thornton, who loathed putting pen to paper, groaned inwardly. She had been a busy bee, epistles to him and Rupert both. With only a bit more effort, she could have produced a horrid mystery.

"The problem is," she was saying, "I do not know his direction." She looked expectantly at him.

"Nor do I."

"You don't!" She was astonished.

"No, sorry. I am certain he did not mention where he was staying when I saw him the other day, and I quite failed to ask him."

"Well, that is most odd." She was looking decidedly annoyed. "You are his guardian, I believe."

"But not his keeper." Even to his own ears he sounded a bit snappish. He modified his tone. "Surely your friends, the Whitfields, will know where he is staying. You might inquire of them."

"Indeed," she sniffed, "I would not dream of doing so."

"I see."

There was heavy silence.

The interview, obviously, had not gone the way young Miss Wentworth had wished. Lord Thornton tried to smooth her ruffled feelings. "It is very thoughtful of you to wish to heal the breach between Rupert and me, but it really isn't necessary. He came to my rooms recently, you see, to apologize for his attack, and I explained then that he had got entirely the wrong idea when he saw us at St. Paul's. He came to understand that I was really trying to prevent your being trampled and not, ah, assaulting your virtue."

"I see," she said in her turn.

"So there is no need for you to contact Rupert. That is, not unless you desire to do so for some other reason."

"Oh, no, of course not," she replied rather sadly. "There could be no other reason."

"I did not think so. For, as I recall, you made it quite plain that you wished no more to do with him."

"Yes, that is true, but —" she hesitated.

"Yes," he prodded, against his better judgment.

"It is just that one cannot help recalling that before that odious elopement, we were the best of friends. It now seems such a pity."

"Yes, but the change is understandable. Even the threat of a marriage, not even to mention the reality, has a way of putting the damper onto friendship. That is why I have been at particular pains to avoid either state."

"Oh, look! There she is!"

Lady Frances Kentmere nudged Mr. Stanesby's arm and pointed. Miss Claudia Wentworth was just turning into the circulating library. "Do you think it will be possible for you to stand here while I jump down and fetch her?"

Mr. Stanesby looked apprehensively at the line of vehicles of all descriptions stretched out behind him and the pair of high-stepping grays pulling a brand-new rig. His heart sank at the prospect. But "Oh, certainly," he said stoutly as he pulled the team to a halt in the middle of Bond Street, accompanied by a chorus of catcalls. He now regretted not ordering his coachman to try out the rig. He could have impressed Lady Frances easier in his curricle. That had been out of the question, though.

"I shall hurry."

Lady Frances suited action to her words as she leapt from the high seat with amazing athleticism and rushed inside just as Major Landseer took Claudia by the arm and was ushering her toward a secluded area. Lady Frances was too single-minded for the significance of this action to register as she swooped down upon them.

"Miss Wentworth, I've found you! Lady Harville said you might be here. Can you come at once? Mr. Stanesby is holding up traffic outside. He is considering buying a new barouche, you see, and wants my approval. I fear" — she smiled apologetically — "that I led Mama to believe you would be along. She is odiously old-fashioned where appearances are concerned. So do come and save my reputation." She suddenly remembered her manners. "Will you not come, too, Major — Landseer, isn't it? I know that Mr. Stanesby would value a man's opinion over ours." She had Claudia by the hand and was pulling her past the crowded shelves toward the door, never doubting her agreeableness.

"Must you go?" Hugo mouthed, and when Claudia nodded, he shrugged his shoulders and followed.

Mr. Stanesby, though relieved to be on his way (hardly more so than the blocked vehicles) was not best pleased to see this addition to his party. He had, in truth, hoped to have Lady Frances to himself, but had accepted with a good grace the need to have Miss Wentworth accompany them. But being saddled with this fellow was a bit too much.

He had taken a dislike to the major at Covent

Garden, though he would have been hard-pressed to say just why. Most likely it was because Thornton obviously didn't care for him, and he always bowed to his friend's superior judgment. And, of course, it did not help matters that the fellow looked like that Adonis cove they went on and on about in the Greek lessons he'd suffered through. But at the moment the thing he most resented was the fact that a cavalryman was bound to know a great deal more about horseflesh than he did and would feel compelled to share his knowledge. He had hoped to impress Lady Frances with his own expertise.

He need not have worried. In fact, he could soon forget that there were passengers behind him, so silent had the two become. He and Lady Frances were able to chatter together without interruption, though she did steal a glance over her shoulder now and then.

Claudia, who had been in something of a daze since crossing Grosvenor Square, an experience similar to crossing the Rubicon, rallied enough to notice that her new friend's expression was disapproving. Only then did she realize that Hugo was sitting improperly close. His thigh was, in fact, pressed warmly against her own. That she had been oblivious to this impropriety said volumes about her state of mind. As she all but leapt away from the close proximity, the barouche turned, none too skillfully, into Hyde Park.

The park was teeming with excitement. Carriages, horsemen, and pedestrians vied with one another for right-of-way. The animated conversation in the driver's seat of their vehicle stopped. Mr. Stanesby had all he could do to control his high-spirited pair in such a hubbub. All at once and unaccountably, carriages and horseback riders began drawing to the side of the road to make a passageway. People on foot were hurrying from all directions, shouting and pointing at some distant target. Parents tightly gripped their children's hands or held the more timid little ones in their arms, keeping their eyes averted.

"My God, what is that?" Mr. Stanesby exclaimed as he managed, with difficulty, to pull his rig to the side of the carriage road behind a four-horse landau crowded with gawkers.

That was a fierce, indeed almost demonic-looking, figure riding a magnificent white horse and flanked by two menacing Cossacks, armed with long and deadly looking spears.

"It's Platov." Major Landseer snapped out of his near sulk to explain.

"Platov! God help us," Mr. Stanesby muttered, and Claudia sloughed off her preoccupation and half rose in her seat to view the exotic that all London talked of.

Chapter Eighteen

All the Russians excited curiosity. But none attracted the kind of attention given to Matvel Platov. Platov was the leader, or "Hetman," of the Don Cossacks, ferocious warriors whose barbarity made them dreaded by friends and foes alike.

Since little factual was known about the man, rumor ran rampant among his English hosts. It was said that even though he looked no more than forty, he was actually sixty-four. It was said that the magnificent animal that he rode was magic. Had it not carried him safely through all of his campaigns? It was also said that he owned twenty thousand horses and could call out an army of vassals eighty thousand strong.

As he galloped past Mr. Stanesby's carriage, the count stared straight ahead, his face reflecting disdain for the crowd that ogled him. It was soon evident, however, that he was not oblivious to his surroundings, for no sooner had he passed the barouche than he reined in his huge white stallion.

"Oh God, he has seen us," the major muttered beneath his breath.

The Cossacks did indeed wheel and ride back toward them while the onlookers craned their necks with curiosity.

The Hetman reined his horse alongside the

carriage while his bodyguard closed in to protect his flank from the curious crowd. His dark eyes flicked quickly over the other occupants of the carriage, then fastened upon Claudia. She felt her color rise under the bold stare, but refused to be outfaced, and stared right back.

What she saw was a trifle disappointing — a rather ordinary-looking man, neither handsome nor homely, with an aquiline nose, pointed chin, and receding hairline. Only his eyes upheld his reputation. Without a doubt he would be a fierce enemy. A fierce suitor as well, her instincts told her.

He snapped a few words in Russian to Major Landseer, who proceeded with obvious reluctance to introduce his party, explaining as he did so "Count Platov speaks no English." Everyone nodded and smiled awkwardly, especially so since the count's eyes never left Claudia's face as he acknowledged the others. After a long, increasingly uncomfortable pause, he spoke a few more words, softly, in his native tongue, then wheeled his horse and galloped away, followed by his guard.

"Whoosh!" Mr. Stanesby let out the breath he had been holding and flicked the reins. "I'd as lief be introduced to a Siberian wolf. The fellow fair gave me the creeps." They began moving with the reactivated traffic. "What did he have to say for himself, anyhow? Dashed if it sounded anything like 'Happy to make your acquaintance' to me."

"Goodness, Miss Wentworth" — Lady Frances turned in her seat — "he certainly seemed taken with you."

Claudia allowed herself a shudder — a reaction she had barely managed to keep in check under the Russian stare. "I quite agree with Mr. Stanesby. He does have a lupine quality."

"You speak the language, Major," Mr. Stanesby persisted, "what did he say?"

The major was slow to reply. It became evident, to Claudia at any rate, that he was seething.

"Yes?" Mr. Stanesby prodded.

"He told Miss Wentworth here that it was their destiny to meet and they would do so again."

"Good heavens!" Lady Frances was appalled.

"Damned foreigner!" Mr. Stanesby growled. "If you ask me, the sooner they all go back where they belong, the better off we'll be. Spears in Hyde Park! Did you ever hear of such a thing?"

Mr. Stanesby kept up a running commentary upon the contribution of the Russians, Austrians, and Prussians in the defeat of Napoleon (meager in his eyes compared to the British) until they had reached Grosvenor Square. The major alighted and assisted Claudia from the carriage. As he escorted her to the door, he said in an undertone, "We must talk. I am in agony every minute that I am near you and cannot say what is in my heart."

"Really, Hugo, that is nonsense. There is nothing to be said."

"Oh, but there is. You must allow me to explain myself. You owe me that much."

Owe him? Owe *him!* She stared up in astonishment, scarcely believing her ears, and was forming a scathing reply when the door began to open.

"Same time tomorrow. The library," he hurriedly whispered as a footman stepped aside to allow Evelina to exit. Hugo turned quickly away and hurried back to the waiting carriage.

Evelina stared wide-eyed after him. "He looked familiar. Who is he?" she asked her aunt.

"A friend of Mr. Stanesby," Claudia prevaricated.

"He is certainly handsome. You might have introduced me, you know."

"Oh, I am sorry. He appeared in a rush. Didn't wish to keep the horses waiting, I expect."

"Well, the next time, present me. I am not a child, you know," and Evelina swept past her, her maid following, in quest of ribbons to make a bonnet, already twice worn, look like new.

Claudia was not aware she had a plan until it was interrupted. But when the butler said that Lady Harville desired to speak with her as soon as she returned, she realized that all she wished to do was seek the solitude of her room and attempt to sort out the happenings of this turbulent day. And had it been anyone besides her hostess, she would have made excuses. But respect and affection made rag-manners impossible. She went immediately to the small parlor.

"Oh, good. You are back." Lady Harville put

down the book she was reading and smiled as Claudia entered. "I must confess, I have been on pins and needles for your return."

"Yes, I can see that." Claudia nodded at the book.

"Do I detect sarcasm? If you had noticed, I was holding it upside down. But never mind all that. I am simply bursting with news. And I think you should sit down to hear it." She indicated a wing-back chair opposite hers.

Claudia sat obediently, wishing herself secure in her bedchamber, back home in Fairwood, in Timbuktu, anywhere but here, forced to face a sit-down-for crisis in this already heavily laden day.

"Oh, my dear, no need to look so stricken. I should have said immediately that this news is good. Marvelous, in fact. You see, I have just received a message from Mr. Edgerton. You remember. The publisher I spoke of. He has read your novel and is most impressed. And" — she clapped her hands with delight — "he wishes to discuss publication!"

The news almost — almost — canceled out all the terrible events of the day.

"Pray forgive me," Lady Harville was saying, "Mr. Edgerton suggested ten o'clock tomorrow, and not knowing whether you would return in time to reply, I took the liberty of saying you would be there. I hope you do not mind my presumption."

"Mind!" Claudia was in transports. She and

Lady Harville chattered excitedly about the upcoming interview — what she should wear, what she should say, what it might mean.

Then much, much later when she was finally in bed and had blown out her candle, she reveled in the delight of this development. A famous publisher had read the story that she had written, and had liked it! Nothing else in her life, she told herself, now mattered except for that one, glorious fact. She had no reason to remember Hugo's soft, pleading eyes. Or the insolent expression of the Russian count as he stared at her. The only event of importance that this day had held was the fact that she now knew she had not been deluding herself. She, Claudia Wentworth, spinster, was also Claudia Wentworth, author.

So why was it that just as she was finally about to drift off to sleep, the memory of a shocking stolen kiss jarred her wide awake again?

Chapter Nineteen

Claudia was not the only member of her family to patronize the library. Evelina, left with more time on her hands since a certain coolness had developed between her and the Miss Whitfields, had discovered horrid mysteries. She was on her way to return *Necromancer of the Black Forest* when she spied her aunt some distance ahead going in the same direction. She considered joining her but was put off by the other's pace. Personally she preferred to stroll, not hurry down the street like a Bow Street Runner after a snatch purse. She resolved to ask, when she did catch up, if the book Claudia carried was overdue. But when, moments later, she followed her aunt inside the lending library, Claudia seemed to have disappeared. Puzzled, Evelina wandered among the shelves until at last she rounded the corner of a back room and spied her aunt standing in a secluded nook, engaged in earnest conversation with a tall, handsome gentleman. Aided by the uniform, Evelina recognized him immediately. He was Mr. Stanesby's friend who had escorted Claudia to the door the day before. She had had only a glimpse of him as he hurried away, but there had been something familiar about him that niggled at her mind. And now, as she stared harder at the well-shaped head bent in earnest conversation — he appeared to be pleading, actually — alarm bells began going off inside her mind. Without quite knowing why, Evelina discarded the notion of joining her aunt. Instead she hurried back around the corner and bumped into a very solid object.

"Rupert!" She managed to reduce a yelp down to a whisper. "What in heaven's name are you doing here?"

"Followed you, didn't I?" he replied in a normal voice till she hissed "Sssh!" and then he, too, whispered. "I saw you come in here unattended. Where the deuce is your maid? This is London, for God's sake. You shouldn't go abroad on your own."

She was only half listening as she peered around the corner once more and saw her aunt and the soldier move her way. "Oh, my goodness!" she gasped. "We must get out of here. Hurry!" She sped toward the door, flinging *Necromancer of the Black Forest* on a table as she left with a bewildered Rupert in her wake.

She turned back the way she had come, and put two buildings between her and the library before halting in front of an apothecary's window. Its contents appeared to fascinate her. "Quick!" she hissed at Rupert, "screen me but with your back toward the library so Claudia doesn't recognize you. I'll peep around you."

"Have you lost your mind?" he demanded as he more or less followed instructions, while staring back over his shoulder.

"Don't look, peagoose, she'll see you!"

Evelina's undertone managed to convey a shriek.

She need not have worried, though. Claudia and the major did not glance their way, but proceeded at a rapid pace in the opposite direction.

"I'll have to follow them," she whispered.

"Then, I'll go with you," he whispered back.

"You will?" The smile she launched his way nearly knocked him off his feet.

They matched their steps to the other couple's rapid progress. The man seemed intent upon wasting no time. He was obviously bent upon making some point as they hurried along. But then they came to a halt in front of a building identified by a discreet sign: THOMAS EDGERTON, PUBLISHER.

Evelina grabbed Rupert's arm to prevent his walking farther. This time he knew the drill and assumed his screening position without prompting, while she peered around him. "I am almost certain now," she whispered.

"Of what?"

"Sssssh — he's leaving!"

Sure enough, when Rupert risked a peek over his shoulder, the soldier was kissing Claudia's hand, perhaps not as lingeringly as he might have wished, for she hastily retrieved it and hurried into the building.

Evelina and Rupert were examining the window display — a rather gross assortment of skinned rabbits and plucked fowl hanging from hooks (enough, to Rupert's mind, to put you off your feed for life), when the major approached. So preoccupied was the military man that he seemed quite unaware of their presence. Evelina took advantage of his preoccupation to stare directly at him as he passed.

"I knew it!" she crowed triumphantly after the major was out of earshot. "It is he all right, and no mistake."

"And just who is he?"

"He is the man in the miniature! I thought he looked familiar when he escorted Claudia home. But I was unable to place him until I saw him again in the library. Then it struck me. He looked exactly like the miniature. Except it can't be. But now that I have had a better look, I am certain that it must be."

"I collect that you know what you are talking about, but you are making no sense to me whatsoever."

"Oh, I am sorry." They had begun walking slowly back toward Grosvenor Square. The major was far ahead by now with the distance between them rapidly increasing. "It is just so absolutely unbelievable that he should be the man in the miniature that it has quite bowled me over."

"I can see that. Now, pray explain before I shake you. What man? What miniature?"

"The one hidden in Aunt Claudia's handkerchief drawer at Fairwood. And before you say anything, I was a small child when I discovered it quite by accident."

"I see. What a remarkable memory you have."

"Oh, very well, then. It wasn't all that long ago." She dimpled, and he laughed. "And I was not prying, actually, but I was borrowing a handkerchief without asking, and I found the miniature wrapped in velvet there in Claudia's drawer. Remember, I told you that when I asked Papa why it was that Claudia never married, he said that she had been betrothed to a soldier when she was very young. But Papa went on to say that the man was posted overseas and never returned. I just assumed, you see, that the man had been killed in battle. Papa forbade me, and he was very stern as I recall, to ever mention the matter to Claudia. But that is the same man. I am positive of it. Can you imagine? Back from the dead and kissing Claudia's hand. Is it not wonderful?" Her eyes were shining as she looked up at Rupert. "Why, it is just like a gothic novel."

"If you say so." He seemed deep in thought.

"I do say so. For in those books people keep popping up unexpectedly after you are made to believe they have perished at sea or whatever. But you never expect such things to happen in real life."

"No, you do not," he said firmly. "And doesn't it seem rather odd that your aunt didn't appear exactly in transports? I had the impression that she really cut short that hand-kissing business."

"Well, yes, now that you mention it, that does seem odd." Evelina descended from her romantic cloud. "And yesterday, too. Why on earth did she not come dancing in singing, 'He is here! Back from the grave!' or some such thing? Claudia did not act the least bit joyous. In fact," she mused, "she seemed upset if anything. Though with my aunt, it is difficult to tell. She does hide her feelings so."

"Unlike some people we know" was Rupert's thought, prudently unuttered.

"And are you absolutely, positively sure that this is the same fellow?" was what he did say.

"Absolutely. Positively."

"Would you like me to investigate? See what I can find out about the cove?"

"Oh, would you?" Her expressive eyes were filled with gratitude. "I am simply dying to know all about him. Only" — she now looked doubtful — "wouldn't that be impossible? I do not even know his name."

"Shouldn't be too difficult. After all, we do know that he is in the Guards, don't we?"

"Of course. I say, you would make a marvelous Bow Street Runner."

But before he had had sufficient time to bask in her admiration, she was struck by another thought. "Of course there are quite a few of them, are there not? And without a name —"

"No problem there. It is a tight-knit society. My brother has close friends in the regiment. I'll get Thorn to introduce me."

"Well," Evelina's enthusiasm was waning; doubt crept into her tone, "I am not sure that you can count on Lord Thornton to know where his friends are. After all, he did not even know your direction."

"That is not so odd, for I have been giving him a wide berth. I am not supposed to be in London, you know." He tried to sound casual, but he could not avoid looking at her suspiciously. "When did you see my brother?"

"Just the other day."

"Indeed?" This time there was no attempt to soften his tone. "You seem to be on quite intimate terms with 'his lordship.'" His brother's title came out as a sneer.

"Me? On intimate terms with Lord Thornton? That is absurd. Why, he is an ancient."

"He ain't that old." He kicked a stone out of their path with a bit more force than necessary. It landed on the portico of the house they were passing. They increased their pace as the door began to open.

"Perhaps not. But even though I should not say so — after all, he is your brother — the truth is, I cannot really like him. And I am certain he does not care for me above half." She was examining his face quizzically. "Do you know something, Rupert? If it were not for how things stand between us now, I would swear that you were jealous."

"Not a bit of it! I just would not like to see you involved with him, that's all. Bound to get hurt. True, he ain't quite as bad as what I called him when I landed the facer." He looked a bit embarrassed at the memory. "But he is a here-and-therein where women are concerned. Can't account for it myself. He's the firstborn. It's his duty to marry. But he is definitely altar-shy."

"There is really no need to warn me off. If you wonder how it happened that I was in your brother's company, I wished him to carry a letter I had written you. But, as I said, he didn't know your direction. Which still seems unbrotherly to me."

"You wrote me a letter?" His eyes widened.

"Yes. You see, I wished to explain the circumstances that led up to the scene you witnessed at St. Paul's. The incident, I mean, that caused you to take exception to your brother's behavior. For you completely mistook the matter. But then, Lord Thornton told me that he had already done so, so I tore my letter up."

"Pity. I should far rather have heard it from you than from him."

They walked on in silence for a bit, then, "How are the Miss Whitfields?" she asked casually.

"I wouldn't know. I have not seen them of late."

"Really? I thought you were always in Mary Whitfield's pocket."

"Well, I'm not."

"If you are avoiding her because of a fear of seeing me, you needn't. I do not see them anymore. At least not if I can help it."

"Why? From fear of seeing me?"

"Actually, if you will not accuse me of being

cattish, the truth is, I do not care for her."

"Can't say that I do, either. But I like her mother even less than that."

They had reached Harville House. He bade her good-bye at the iron gateway. "Thank you for everything," she said formally. He tipped his hat just as politely and turned away.

"Oh, Rupert!" she called impulsively when he had walked only a yard or so. He turned to face her. "If I have messed up your life in any way, I deeply regret it. Pray tell me that I have not."

He frowned and seemed to think it over carefully before he spoke.

"Oh, I do believe that you have done just that, Evelina. Probably past all redemption."

Chapter Twenty

From the moment that Claudia left the house to keep her appointment with the publisher, Lady Harville had been on pins and needles. She had made countless trips to the upstairs window to stare futilely down Grosvenor Street. When at last she spied her friend approaching, she hurried to the entryway to greet her.

"I have had tea prepared," she said as the front door closed behind Claudia. "We must have a comfortable coze while you tell me everything that happened. I can hardly wait to hear. I will not even allow you to go to your bedchamber to remove your bonnet. You must do it in the drawing room.

"Oh, dear."

For the first time, as they sat across the tea table from one another and Claudia was untying bonnet strings while her hostess poured the tea, Lady Harville took time to study her friend's face. "You are a master, my dear — or mistress, I should say — at disguising your true feelings. But now even I can see that something is amiss. Do not tell me that Mr. Edgerton does not like your novel. After the letter he wrote, I will not believe it."

"Oh, he claims to like it very much indeed."

"What, then? He does not wish to publish it?

But that makes no sense whatsoever."

"Oh, he is quite eager to publish it. Or so he says. At my expense."

"Oh, dear."

Lady Harville fell back once more upon that inadequate expression. She was, in truth, shocked by the bitterness of Claudia's tone. "I am so very sorry that it could not have been otherwise, but it is my understanding, dear, that this is not an unusual arrangement for first authors. The authoress of *Sense and Sensibility* paid for its publication, I am told."

"So Mr. Edgerton said."

"If it is a matter of finances," Lady Harville offered delicately, "you know how greatly I admire your book."

"You are very kind." Claudia managed a grateful smile. "But that is not it, you see. I think I could possibly manage the thing myself. And if not, once Edwin got over the shock that I have done such an unladylike thing as to pen a novel, I am sure he would finance it. But that is not the point, you see."

"And the point is?" Lady Harville prodded gently.

"It was foolish of me. I can see that now. But I had hoped for more than just the gratification of having actually written a novel — which is not to say that I am not inordinately proud of having done so. But my wishful thinking was that I could gain independence through my writing. As I said, it was very foolish of me. Now, if you will excuse me" — Claudia managed another, weaker, smile — "I plan to go to my chamber, have a fit of the sulks, then lick my wounds and be better company when next you see me."

After her friend had gone, Lady Harville sat in deep thought. Her heart ached for Claudia. She had had to bite her tongue to keep from offering more arguments in favor of accepting Mr. Edgerton's offer. And from pointing out that any advance of capital on her part would be of short duration. For such a wonderful story was bound to sell well. But she had not tried to influence Claudia. Better to let her have her "fit of the sulks" as she called it. Time was a healer. Perhaps it could serve to temper Claudia's stiff pride.

When her butler appeared to tell her that Lord Thornton had called, she was glad for the diversion. She, as well as Claudia, needed cheering up.

But it was soon evident that his lordship was not to be cast in the role of cheerer. To say he was blue-deviled did not begin to describe his mood. He came perilously close to being in a temper. He could not stop berating himself for his rackety conduct. What had possessed him to make love to Miss Wentworth in a public place — or in a private place, if it came to that? He had no answer. He must be dicked in the nob. There was no other explanation.

And as if that were not enough, the last straw had been his brother's visit. Rupert had just seen

Claudia tête-à-tête with the pretty major, and wished to make inquiries about him. Would Thornton supply a note of introduction to a Guardsman friend who might know his history?

"Why are you so interested in Miss Wentworth's affairs?" Thornton had asked.

The question seemed a reasonable one. Rupert was evasive. "The cove looks like a miniature that Evelina once showed me of Miss Wentworth's fiancé. Except he was supposed to have been killed in the war. But if this isn't the same fellow, then it has to be his twin. I'm just curious, that's all," he finished lamely.

His older brother did not believe the explanation for a minute. He was about to quiz him further, then considered enlightening Rupert himself, then changed his mind on both counts and gave him Colonel McKinney's direction instead.

But Claudia's tryst with that married military philanderer incensed him. She would say it was none of his concern, and she was right, of course. But, damn it all, he had thought her a woman of sense. There was a contradiction of terms, by George!

So all in all he did not present a sunny countenance to Lady Harville as she received him in the drawing room. He declined a chair and, in exchange for her greeting, came directly to the point. "Sorry, but I will not be able to escort you to Almack's. I have a prior commitment."

Lady Harville looked at him shrewdly. "I see," she said, and actually appeared to. "We would enjoy your company of course. But I quite understand that I have monopolized a great deal of your time already. And to little avail, I fear." She smiled ruefully up at him. "I must confess that I have been matchmaking. Again. I had thought Lady Frances would be perfect for you. But now it appears that Cupid's arrows have struck her and your friend, Mr. Stanesby. Well, at least I did not entirely waste my time," she chuckled. "He seems like a very nice young man, though rather weak in the intellect for her, I fear. But still — there is no accounting for love, is there?"

"I wouldn't know," he growled, "and would prefer to keep it that way.

"As for Almack's, I am sure the two of them could escort you and Miss Wentworth. Where is she, by the by?"

"She is lying down. Or so I believe." She hesitated a moment, than added, "I fear she is rather upset."

He looked uncomfortable. "I am not surprised."

"You are not? Then, you know about her book? I had thought I was her only confidant."

"Book? What book? I have not the slightest notion what you mean."

"Oh, dear. Then, I have let the cat out of the bag. Thornton, do stop your pacing and sit down. You are making me dizzy.

"Now, you must promise not to repeat a word of this," she continued when he had taken the chair Claudia had recently vacated.

"Well, I would be hard-pressed to do so, ma'am, since, as I said, you are making no sense whatsoever."

"Promise, and I will explain."

"I'm no gossipmonger, but if you must have a pledge, so be it."

She went on then to tell him of Claudia's disappointing interview with the publisher and the rejection of her own offer to help.

For one of the few times in his life, Lord Thornton was speechless.

"A lady author. Good God!" he finally managed.

"Is that so alarming? They are becoming almost commonplace these days. And surely it cannot be wonderful that a woman should have as much imagination as a man."

"Or more. Much, much more. I certainly grant you that. But —"

"But what?" she frowned.

"My word," he stared at her curiously, "you are prickly on this subject, are you not?"

"It is a marvelous book." She poured cold tea for the both of them and sipped hers unconciously.

"I do not doubt it for a minute."

"Well, you should not. That is what distressed me, you see. Miss Wentworth's book is superior to anything Fanny Burney has written, for example. That is why it is so mean-spirited of Mr. Edgerton to ask her to pay for publication. Why, he is sure to make a profit."

"And she absolutely refused to let you assist her?"

"Would not hear of it. But I am hoping that after she calms down a bit, she will see reason and accept my offer. It is all a matter of pride, you see. Not only does she consider this a reflection upon the merits of her work, she feels a door has been closed. She had hoped, you see, for financial independence."

"Indeed? I had no idea that Miss Wentworth was without funds. Is her brother tightfisted, then? I am not amazed. He struck me as a most unpleasant sort."

"Oh, Sir Edwin is not all that bad when one gets to know him. Merely old-fashioned. All the money is in his hands, you see, and though she is certain he would give her anything else within his power — including a handsome dowry — he is adamantly opposed to her setting up her own household."

"I see."

He sat in thought a moment. "How little one knows of one's acquaintances. Miss Wentworth, the writer. I confess to being amazed." He took a sip of tea and grimaced.

"As I said, Claudia is quite reticent on the subject. Even her family does not know. You could hardly have expected her to confide in a mere acquaintance."

"A mere acquaintance? I think not."

"Well, I suppose that haring off in the night after your eloping relatives in such a shocking manner did put your relationship into a different category. Though what that category would be defies imagination. At any rate I cannot conceive of you and her having a comfortable coze about literature."

"Nor can I. But you do say the book is good?"

"Excellent."

"Tell me about it."

"I will do nothing of the kind. For I refuse to abandon hope of its publication. Then, you can read it for yourself."

"Not likely."

"Oh? That high-toned public school of yours failed to teach you to read, did it?"

"Very amusing. I do read, it happens. But gothic novels are hardly in my style."

"Pity. For I think this one would capture your interest. There is a character in it that puts me very much in mind of you."

"You're funning!"

"I am serious."

"Really? The hero?"

"Certainly not. The villain."

"Oh well, then. That is all right. Had me worried for a bit."

Her laughter was interrupted by the butler announcing morning callers. Thornton rose to leave.

"Oh, by the by," he said casually when he reached the door. "Miss Wentworth's hero. Is he by chance devilishly handsome, tall, with fair hair?"

"Why, of course. How else should a proper English hero look?"

He grunted with disgust.

Lady Harville smiled to herself as the door closed behind him.

Lord Thornton walked slowly down Grosvenor Street, deep in thought. Almost by accident his direction led to Whitehall, where he turned into the offices of Thomas Edgerton, publisher.

Chapter Twenty-one

"Almack's is a must," Lady Harville had declared. "Though," she added with a twinkle, "I would be willing to wager that once you have been there, you will wonder why that is so. But no matter how dull you may find it, I would be most derelict in my duty as hostess if I did not take you there. And in years to come," she declaimed, like an actor center stage, "when you are an old, old lady and the subject of the famous assembly rooms is raised, as of course it will be, you can say 'Ah, yes, I know. I was there.' "

"My goodness" — Claudia laughed — "you make it sound as if I had fought at Agincourt."

"Oh, that would not be nearly so prestigious as Almack's, I am sure."

Claudia, who had no interest whatsoever in going to the famous assembly rooms, was at some pains not to show it. For she was well aware of the honor being paid her. Almack's was known as the "seventh heaven of the fashionable world." It was the feminine equivalent of the famous Gentlemen's Clubs of London. The very word, "Almack's," had come to be synonymous with exclusivity.

The assemblies were ruled with iron hands by a group of patronesses who issued vouchers only to the crème de la crème of the fashionable world. No one in "trade" need even hope. Young ladies suffered and wept if not included, for as Henry Luttrell pointed out in his satirical verse:

> All on that magic list depends;
> Fame, fortune, fashion, lovers, friends.

"Oh, I should give anything — *anything* to be going!" Evelina had exclaimed when she learned of her aunt's invitation. So it seemed there was no way Claudia could be so rag-mannered as to cry off, even though she longed to. It was especially important to appear agreeable, since it was rumored that on this particular evening the czar would be there.

"Oh, my dear, you do look lovely!"

On the appointed night Lady Harville, elegant herself in black crepe over sarcenet with a white crepe toque covering her hair, smiled her approval when Claudia joined her in the withdrawing room to await their escort.

"Oh, you do!" Evelina had told the ladies that they did not dare leave without showing off their finery. She now drank in the details of the white lace over white satin evening gown her aunt was wearing. Its corsage of pale rose satin, cut low to expose more bosom than Claudia was comfortable with showing, was lavishly trimmed with pearls. More pearls and satin roses ornamented her upswept hair. "I am not used to seeing you look quite so — so — exquisite."

"My goodness," Claudia laughed, "I am not sure if I have been complimented or insulted. But, at any rate, I am pleased you admire my gown."

"Oh, it is not only the gown, though I do like it above all things. Do you suppose that I could wear it?"

"Certainly. When you are twenty-seven."

"Actually, I was thinking more of my come-out. That is," she added disconsolately, "if I ever have such a thing."

Fortunately, before Evelina could dampen the festive mood that even Claudia was beginning to feel, they were interrupted by the arrival of their escort.

Sir Malcomb Martingale was an old, old friend of Lady Harville who, so it was rumored, would have liked to be much closer and therefore proposed marriage periodically. He was a small man, had kept his figure, and while not precisely handsome, he was quite distinguished-looking with a thatch of white hair and a face whose network of lines not only betrayed age but added character. All in all, their party managed to turn heads as they alighted from their carriage in front of the assembly rooms.

Crowds had gathered in the streets awaiting the arrival of the royal Russians. Sir Malcomb and the ladies were forced to stand outside the building while the czar's party made its entrance. When she spied Count Platov among the Russian entourage, Claudia managed to hide behind a tall and portly gentleman. Her spirits sank even lower. Hugo was in the party. He looked even more handsome than usual in his dress uniform — a feat she would have thought impossible. It was just as impossible to interpret the various feelings that the sight of him aroused. The one thing she was sure of was that she had no wish to sort those feelings out on such a night.

At last they were able to make their way into the anteroom. "Oh, there is Thornton," Lady Harville exclaimed. And sure enough Claudia could see the familiar dark head preceding them in the crowd. With difficulty, she suppressed a sigh. Her hard-won pleasure in the evening was fast evaporating. Almack's, it appeared, was well supplied with those persons whom she wished particularly to avoid.

Despite Lady Harville's warning, she was quite disappointed with the ballroom. Statues and plasterwork adorned the walls, as did large gilded mirrors placed there to reflect the glow of several two-tiered chandeliers that shed light and occasionally tallow upon the finely arrayed guests. The musicians' balcony had been enhanced with a patterned design; swatches of gold tasseled velvet dressed the tops of the tall windows. Even so, the overall effect was rather drab. She had seen grander assembly rooms in the provinces.

Sir Malcomb practically raced his guests to three empty chairs before they could be claimed by others in the milling crowd. "We shall have a prime vantage point," he observed when they were seated below the musicians' gallery. "It is rumored that they plan to dance that shocking new dance everyone talks of. What is it called, m'dear?" He turned to Lady Harville.

"The waltz. And, I must confess, I am dying to see it."

"You, too, eh?" he answered with a twinkle. "Well, it is obvious that we are all being corrupted by this foreign invasion. England will never be the same. Oh, I say. There is Thornton, But who is the beauty with him?"

Both his companions turned to stare down the ballroom in the direction he had indicated. Lord Thornton, accompanied by a tall, striking, chestnut-haired lady wearing a gown that caused Claudia suddenly to feel dowdy, was listening to Mr. Stanesby expound upon some subject that evidently required a great deal of gesticulation on his part. Lady Frances, who looked splendid in white gauze with an ostrich plume adorning her hair, and Lord Thornton's companion were in quieter conversation.

"Who is she? The one with Thornton?" Sir Malcomb repeated as he squinted toward the group through his quizzing glass.

"Lady Sophia Carstairs."

There was something a bit repressive in Lady Harville's tone.

If Claudia's attention had not been riveted already, that name would have done the trick. As it was, the level of her attention rose several notches.

"Indeed? Didn't recognize her," Sir Malcomb was saying. "Haven't seen her since she married her doddering old husband. Don't suppose he is here."

"I very much doubt it," Lady Harville said dryly. "He spends most of his time in the country, they say."

"Well, they don't say that about his wife," Sir Malcomb chuckled. "From what I hear, she goes about enough for the two of them."

All this attention must have affected its target, for Thornton turned and looked their way and said a few words to his companions. Then he and Lady Carstairs began to elbow through the crush.

"Looks as though we're being honored with a visit," Sir Malcomb murmured as he was rising to his feet.

Claudia had been too busy memorizing every feature of the lady with Lord Thornton to really look at him. Now as the couple approached, she was struck by how well he looked. Evening clothes became him. The black and white severity suited his dark coloring, and though she shocked herself by such inappropriate thoughts, she had to admit that his muscular calves and thighs were well suited to the satin breeches and white silk stockings that hugged him like a second skin.

He bowed as he reached their chairs. "Let's see," he addressed his companion, "you and Lady Harville are known to one another, I collect. May I present Miss Wentworth, Lady Harville's houseguest. Miss Wentworth, Lady Carstairs. And you must surely know Sir Malcomb. Everyone does."

After general polite acknowledgments of the perfunctory introduction, Lady Harville asked after the health of Lady Carstairs's mother. The two were old acquaintances it seemed.

During a lengthy description of his companion's parent's megrims, staggers, rheumatism, and "sudden" teeth, Lord Thornton stood staring down at Claudia. She felt her cheeks grow hot under the intense scrutiny and shot him a glare that seemed to break the spell. "You are looking amazingly well tonight," he murmured. Like Evelina, he sounded a bit surprised.

"Thank you. I think."

There was a bit of asperity in her tone. She was becoming weary of left-handed compliments.

Lady Carstairs had wound up her list of symptoms, and was beginning to cast speaking looks at her escort that he was slow to recognize. But then he appeared to drag himself back from some private reflection, and they took their leave.

"Handsome woman," Sir Malcomb observed as the orchestra above them began to tune their instruments. "Did not Thornton dangle after her a bit before she married old Carstairs?"

"I collect it was more the other way around." It was obvious that Lady Harville did not care for Lady Carstairs.

"Tell me," Claudia could not stop herself from asking, "I believe you said that Lady Carstairs's given name is Sophia. Is she sometimes known as Sophy?"

"Heavens, I hope not," Lady Harville shuddered. "I would not wish that on anyone. But why do you ask?"

Fortunately the orchestra launched loudly into a country-dance and prevented the necessity of an answer.

Lady Harville, stating emphatically that her dancing days were over, insisted that Sir Malcomb partner her guest instead. As they took their places in the set, Claudia, not usually self-conscious, felt that all eyes were upon her. A quick survey of the ballroom assured her that this was not the case. Lord Thornton and Lady Carstairs were in another set as was Hugo, partnering a lady whom she did not recognize, but assumed must be a member of the Russian party. Her eyes moved on to fasten upon the czar and his sister seated near the exit. Alexander was listening attentively to whatever Princess Esterhazy, one of the patronesses, was saying while his sister looked characteristically bored. Claudia, amused to have observed the grand duchess living up to her reputation, was about to glance away when she discovered the source of her unease. Count Platov was standing with folded arms against the wall behind the Russian ruler's party. His fierce eyes were fixed upon her. When he realized he was observed, he did not change expression but bowed in her direction. Claudia pretended not to see him and quickly turned away, not quite able to repress a shudder.

"Are you cold, my dear?" Sir Malcomb inquired solicitously.

"Oh, no." Fortunately, he did not require more explanation.

She could have wished this dance to last forever. All too soon the music stopped. She saw Hugo standing by Lady Harville, waiting to claim her hand, and did not know whether to be sorry or relieved. She had determined to avoid her former fiancé, but he now seemed preferable to the alternatives.

As they took their places in the following set, she was not so sure. Hugo's palm felt warm even within the white gloves he wore, and it was difficult to ignore the squeezes he gave her hand whenever they were separated and reunited by the dance. More disturbing, he kept whispering tenderly in her ear at every opportunity, possibly attempting to make love, but if so his efforts were wasted, for they had had the misfortune to join a set that included Thornton and an unknown partner. Between Platov's impaling gaze from across the room and his lordship's mocking look whenever they came together, she was hard-pressed not to scream. In future years would the name Almack's be inexorably linked with her burning desire for the orchestra balcony to collapse? she wondered.

The music did stop at last (without peril to the

musicians) but once again it was a case of going from bad to worse. Hugo, it seemed, had no intention of escorting her to her chair, only to the edge of the dance floor. "Unless the rules have changed in my absence," he murmured tenderly, "it is quite proper for us to stand up twice."

"I'm not sure it is proper for us to stand up even once," she replied, and tried unsuccessfully to walk away. It would have required a scene to free herself from the firm grip upon her arm.

"Don't be so cruel, dearest heart. I know you have every right to despise me. But I also know you are the only woman I have truly loved."

"Stop it!" she said between clinched teeth, trying to get her message across and look pleasant at the same time, no mean achievement.

"Oh, I know this is neither the time nor place, but when else, pray? Every time I think I shall have a chance to see you alone, to explain myself, I am thwarted. I shall go mad soon if I cannot —"

Whatever Hugo had been about to say was cut short by a preemptory cough. Count Platov had materialized behind them. Claudia barely managed not to jump out of her skin.

The count addressed the British major in barked Russian. It could, as far as she could tell, have been an order to attack the musician's gallery. She hoped it was. The major, who looked decidedly out of countenance, seemed to have no choice other than translate. "Count Platov requests the honor of this dance, Miss Wentworth," he said woodenly.

And at that very moment, the musicians launched into a waltz.

Bless the band! The rescuing cavalry had come galloping over the hill and provided her with a legitimate excuse. She was saved.

"Oh, it is the waltz," she said happily while trying to appear regretful. "Pray thank him for the honor, but explain that I do not know how to waltz."

Hugo, looking quite as relieved as she, turned to relay the message.

The Russian's expression was as unintelligible as the brief words he spoke.

Hugo was perspiring a bit when he translated once again. "He says that he will teach you."

"Oh, but —"

It was too late to protest in any language. The Cossack was propelling her onto the ballroom floor.

Claudia had never even seen a waltz performed, let alone participated. She had heard a great deal about it, of course. It was quite popular in Europe, but the English had always considered it rather shocking, just one more example of continental decadence. And that it should be danced at Almack's, that bastion of strict propriety, seemed unthinkable. Surely the orchestra was only showing off its skill. It would soon be forced to change its tune, for, see, thank goodness, no one was dancing. But then Claudia saw the reason for the delay. Czar Alexander himself was taking the floor, escorting the Princess Esterhazy.

Description had not prepared her for Count Platov's hand upon her waist. "Why, he might as well embrace me," was her shocked response. His thoughts, judging from his wolfish smile, were running along some similar line.

The music now began in earnest, and she was sent spinning around the floor. From that moment on it was a matter of survival, trying to maintain her balance while keeping her feet out from under the Russian dancing pumps. It was clear that Count Platov viewed the waltz in terms of a cavalry charge, the object of which was to ride through or over all enemy opposition. Alert couples parted like swinging gates as they lunged through them; the oblivious suffered the shock of a whirling collision. Through it all the count kept murmuring in her ear — dance instructions, she surmised, for judging from the cadence, it might have been the Russian words for one-two-three, one-two-three. If he was trying to be helpful, she wished that he would think again. All that heavy breathing was the outside of enough.

She was also aware that they were the center of attention. This was the effect that Platov customarily produced, of course, so perhaps it was not really caused by the ineptitude of her performance. Astonishment was the reaction written upon most faces they swooped past. With the exception of Lord Thornton's. That gentleman clearly was amused.

"Thank you, God," she breathed silently when the music finally ceased. She was breathless. She was overheated. From exertion and embarrassment and not, as the Russian obviously thought, from his heavy breathing in her ear. She would never hear a waltz played again without a shudder. Of that much she was sure. But at least the ordeal was over and could now be packed away with scores of other unpleasant memories from her life. She started to move gratefully from the floor and was held once again in an iron grip.

"Please excuse me, but our dance has ended." She smiled politely, and he smiled back. Or at least his lips performed what might have been intended for that expression. But the grip on her arm did not slacken. Claudia looked desperately around for Hugo to break the language barrier and translate her wishes. But he appeared to have left her to her fate.

"Take your places, Ladies and Gentlemen, for the quadrille," the master of ceremonies directed, and the music began once more. "Well, at least this should be an improvement on the waltz," she thought with resignation but was soon made to question her optimism. Count Platov somehow contrived to turn even this into intimacy, standing much too close, keeping his fierce eyes fastened upon her when the figures of the dance forced them apart. The evening was taking on a nightmarish quality. When the quadrille ended, she braced herself for the worst.

The worst happened. Count Platov still would not allow her to leave the dance floor.

"Excuse me, sir, but it is not considered proper in this country to dance more than twice with the same partner," she explained politely and unintelligibly.

He replied perfunctorily in Russian. Her best guess was "I don't give a fig for your customs."

She looked imploringly toward the master of ceremonies for help. It was his duty to see that decorum was maintained. Sure enough, he was looking their way. But then, who wasn't? He was obviously too intimidated by the fierce Cossack to interfere. And as for that frail reed, Major Landseer —

"I believe this is our dance, Miss Wentworth."

Lord Thornton had appeared beside her and was holding out his hand. She had never been so glad to see anyone in all her life. "Oh, yes, it is!"

The problem was that Count Platov's grip increased. To the point of causing pain. He was glaring at Lord Thornton, the same barbaric blaze that had put fifty thousand Frenchmen into flight.

Thornton's reaction was to take Claudia's other hand. "I am about to be pulled apart like a wishbone," she thought with a resignation born of embarrassment and fright. "Perhaps it is just as well."

"I say there, you Russian Son of the Steppes." Lord Thornton spoke softly, but his eyes could have routed their own share of Frenchmen. "You let go of the lady's hand immediately before I mill you down upon the dance floor and not only cause an international incident, but get us both barred from Almack's for life."

The Russian could not have understood a word Lord Thornton said. But the steel in his lordship's eyes spoke a universal language. They were at an impasse, tension-filled. Then with a shrug, Count Platov surrendered. He released Claudia's hand, bowed stiffly, and spit out a few apparently well-chosen words at his adversary.

"Why, yes. I do agree, wholeheartedly," Thornton replied pleasantly. "Your servant, sir." He bowed and smiled and led Claudia from the dance floor.

"What in the world did he just say to you?" she whispered when they were out of earshot.

"That you are easily the most beautiful woman in the room, and that I am something unrepeatable for taking you away from him."

"He said that?" she gasped in astonishment before her numbed brain reactivated. "You are bamming me, of course. You do not understand one word of Russian."

"Oh well, then," he grinned, "have it your own way. I do know that it is what he should have said."

Chapter Twenty-two

It was time to go — for the foreign visitors and for the Wentworth ladies. London would be glad to see the former leave, and Lady Harville urged the latter to stay longer.

Even though she did not doubt the sincerity of the invitation, Claudia had no wish to wear out their welcome. So it was decided that there would be one last hurrah, a visit to Hyde Park. For the Regent had proclaimed that from the first of August, end-of-the-war celebrations would be held in Green, St. James's, and Hyde Parks. There were to be fireworks, towers, pagodas, oriental temples, transfigurations — even a mock naval battle on the Serpentine. It would never do, Lady Harville insisted, to miss so much excitement. But after this, the Wentworths would leave for home.

Even Evelina did not protest the departure. She appeared to have had her fill of the Metropolis and had withdrawn into her shell again. It seemed the London holiday had not been the cure-all that Claudia had hoped for.

As to its effect upon herself — well, she concluded, she would have the rest of her life to sort that out. Without a doubt it had been a high adventure. But at what cost? The dashing of her literary hopes, temporarily at any rate. The shock of seeing Hugo once again after finally — almost? — having put his ghost to rest. And of course there was Lord Thornton. But there was no way she would ever sort that one out.

It was two mornings after the Almack's debacle when the three ladies of Harville House were at breakfast, lost in their own thoughts, that the butler entered carrying three messages upon a silver tray. Two were for the elder Miss Wentworth, the other for the younger. The recipients might just as well have exchanged two of the letters, the contents were so similar. In essence they read: am desperate to see you, name the place. One was signed Hugo. Rupert had prudently left his unsigned. Claudia repressed a sigh as she refolded Hugo's ardent pleading. She would write him, she supposed, to say that any further assignations between them were out of the question. But that could wait. She really was not up to thinking about it now. She broke the seal upon the other letter. Her eyes scanned its contents, then blinked several times to be sure they were in focus. She read it carefully again.

And let out a war whoop.

Lady Harville dropped *The Quarterly Review* she was reading. Evelina choked upon a light wig.

"What on earth has got into you, Claudia?" she asked crossly when she had sufficiently recovered. "Are you dicked in the nob or something?"

"No. Or yes, possibly. And, pray, do not use cant phrases.

"Oh, Lady Harville, the most glorious news! You will not believe it."

"Allow me to try," the older woman smiled.

"This is from Mr. Edgerton." She waved the letter in the air. "He has reconsidered. He wishes to go ahead with publication and is willing to pay me one hundred and ten pounds!"

Lady Harville's whoop was only slightly less Mohican-like than Claudia's.

Evelina stared, openmouthed, from one lady to the other. "Would someone pray tell me what this is all about?"

Both shared the explanation. Sometimes simultaneously; sometimes finishing sentences for one another. To her credit, Evelina sorted the whole thing out.

"You, an authoress!" She stared at her aunt admiringly. "You really are the deep one, are you not? I knew, of course, that you were always scribbling. But I supposed you were merely keeping a diary or writing letters. A novel! Just imagine! Oh, I can hardly wait to read it! And to hear what Papa has to say." She giggled. "The news will send him straight up into the boughs."

The breakfast group at last broke up. Evelina had her note to answer. Claudia planned to dash directly to Whitehall and work out the details of her contract with Mr. Edgerton. Both Wentworths excused themselves. Lady Harville, however, chose to linger longer in the breakfast parlor. She poured herself another cup of tea and sipped it thoughtfully. At last she came to a resolution. She rose from the breakfast table and went directly to her bedchamber desk. There she penned a note of her own, which she immediately dispatched by one of her footmen. In it she made it clear she would brook no excuses. Lord Thornton was commanded to serve her and her party as escort to Hyde Park.

The park had been transformed. And not for the better, her ladyship observed. And many Londoners agreed, fearing it would never be the same again. Indeed, it more closely resembled the Sahara than the lovely verdant pleasure ground it once had been. No vestige of grass remained. An excess of visitors all summer long had seen to that. Booths and makeshift taverns stretched for two whole miles. The Serpentine had lost its tranquil look and was now crowded with mock battleships. The once-clear air was filled with the stench of tobacco, liquors, and unwashed bodies.

After the initial shock was worked through by many exclamations and much discussion, the group from Grosvenor Square suspended criticism and entered into the spirit of the day. Lord Thornton, conscripted into squiring his aunt and her houseguests, had expanded the party to include Lady Frances Kentmere and Mr. Stanesby. They were all more than willing to wander through the crowds, examine the wares in the booths, applaud the fire-eaters and the acrobats, and wait for the mock sea battle and the fireworks to begin.

They had started out their strolling as a tight-knit group. But the crowds soon made this formation difficult. Lord Thornton and his aunt were the first to separate. He suspected that a bit of adroit maneuvering on her part had achieved their detachment.

The moment they were out of earshot of the others, Lady Harville confirmed his suspicion. She was examining an assortment of souvenirs that overflowed the rickety shelves of a rickety booth when she remarked a bit too casually, "You paid for Miss Wentworth's book to be published, did you not?"

His bewildered expression was worthy of that great tragedian, Edmund Kean. "What do you mean? I haven't the faintest idea what you are talking about."

"Come, now. You cannot pull the wool over my eyes so easily." They left the booth and walked on slowly. "It appears more than a coincidence that right after I had told you about Claudia's disappointment, her publisher had a change of heart."

"Did he, by Jove! Going to publish Miss Wentworth's book, you say? Well, that is good news."

She sighed with exasperation. "There is no point in maintaining your charade, Thornton. I know that you are responsible. What I do not know is why."

He grinned wryly and capitulated. "Damned if I do, either. Let me make a bargain with you, Aunt. Don't you tell Miss Wentworth that I financed her great work and —"

"As if I would!" she interrupted indignantly. "Why, she would never forgive you."

"I am well aware of that." He gave a Kean-like shudder. "But, as I was saying, if you keep my secret from her, then I will keep yours."

"Mine? I have no secrets from Claudia."

"Indeed? Then, I collect it is perfectly all right for me to let her know that you have been throwing her at my head."

Just then a large young man in pursuit of a small child who had tugged free of his hand careened into them. "Beg pardon, sir." Thornton nodded understandingly, and Lady Harville took a firmer grip upon his arm.

"Throwing Miss Wentworth at your head?" she repeated. "What an absurdity. I did no such thing. As you recall, I did plead guilty to trying to match you with Lady Frances. But that certainly turned out disappointingly. For me, if not for Lady Frances. For of course your dim-witted friend is the soul of amiability. A rare quality in a husband."

"Fustian."

"No, indeed. I assure you that an even temper is a pearl above price in the state of matrimony."

"You know perfectly well what I mean, Machiavelli. Your shameless use of Lady Frances was only a diversionary tactic to draw my attention away from your real plan of attack. You intended Miss Wentworth for me from the first moment you two met. Come now, madam, admit it."

"Why, you puffed-up, conceited —" She had begun to sputter when his roguish expression stopped her. "Oh, very well, then," she laughed. "I am quite caught out. Now the question is, did it work?"

Chapter Twenty-three

Claudia and Evelina had tactfully allowed the distance to grow between Lady Frances and Mr. Stanesby and themselves. But so engrossed were the couple with one another that Claudia doubted the lovers even noticed that they were gone. Any more than Evelina seemed to be aware of her.

Claudia had made at least three comments having to do with the sights around them that got no reaction or reply at all. She was beginning to be somewhat alarmed about the state of her niece's hearing when she spied the source of Evelina's distraction.

A young man in a brown coat, fawn waistcoat, and white trousers, with a black top hat worn low upon his forehead was obviously following them, skulking along behind other pedestrians, dodging into tent openings, and quickly turning his back when she looked his way.

"I do believe that Rupert is trying to get your attention," Claudia said dryly.

This time her niece heard. "Rupert? Rupert Hunt, you mean? Oh, is he here?"

"Yes. As you well know."

"Oh, dear. This is not working at all as planned. I had hoped to be able to slip unobtrusively away. Oh, please, Claudia. May I speak to him? It is most imperative that I do so. And not at all improper. For it has nothing to do with the two of us, I can assure you."

Claudia's lips were in the very act of forming a firm "no" when she hesitated. Just why she did so was beyond all understanding. Perhaps it was because she was too happy over the success of her book to wish to distress anybody else. Or perhaps it was the memory of all those wasted years pining over Hugo. Or perhaps it was the thought that this was the end of their London interlude and would have no bearing upon her niece's life back at Fairwood. Oh, botheration! She quit perhapsing. "Very well," she heard herself saying, "go ahead. But only for a few moments mind you. I will wait right here." She nodded at a nearby bench where a fat lady was munching apples from a basket on her lap.

"Oh, bless you! You are capital!"

Evelina took to her heels while Claudia joined the fat lady on the iron bench and tried not to think what her brother would have to say about such chaperonage.

"Pssst!" Rupert hissed from behind a bush as Evelina hurried past him. "I'm here."

"No need to skulk." Evelina unthinkingly had begun to whisper before changing to a normal tone. "I have my aunt's permission to meet you."

"You have?" He looked amazed as he stepped into the open.

"Yes, but not for long. So we must hurry."

They walked swiftly away, as though speed

would lengthen their time together.

"Well, Miss Wentworth wouldn't have been so free with her permission if she knew why I wished to see you," Rupert said darkly. "One of the reasons, anyhow," he amended.

"Oh, dear." She looked at him anxiously. His frown was thunderous. "You must have found out something dreadful."

"Well, you won't like it above half. I know I didn't."

"Oh, my heavens. I was afraid of this. The major is married, isn't he?"

Rupert looked rather taken down to have had his big news preempted. "Yes, but how did you know?"

"Intuition, I collect. The more I thought on it, the more it stood to reason. Why else would he just disappear out of her life? If he is not dead, he must be married."

"Some alternative," Rupert chuckled.

"Oh, but it is not funny. In fact, it is dreadful."

"True. And you ain't even heard the worst of it. I know I shouldn't be telling you this. Not the proper thing for the ears of a young lady."

"Oh, pooh," Evelina interrupted. "After all we've been through together, you surely aren't going to stand on points with me."

"No, I ain't. For I think your aunt will need to know. Colonel McKinney — he's Thornton's friend and in Landseer's regiment — says that the major deliberately, uh, 'took advantage of,' this Russian diplomat's daughter, who's a real antidote according to the colonel, and got her in the family way so she'd have to marry him."

Evelina stopped stock-still to the peril of the folk behind her. "How awful," she gasped. "Did he — ah — er — ?"

"Rape her?" Rupert said bluntly but in a whisper. "No need for that, I collect. Well, you've seen him. And they do say his wife dotes on him. She's in the family way again, by the by. No, it was her father who objected. But then, when it came down to it, he had to put a best face on the situation and get them to church."

"A Russian objected to an Englishman?" Evelina sniffed. "How very odd."

"Well, he knew that Landseer's a fortune hunter, didn't he?"

"So that was it. She is rich, then?"

"Beyond belief."

"Well, that explains that. Aunt Claudia has very little money of her own. But now what are we to do?"

"I think you will have to tell her."

Evelina sighed heavily. "I was afraid you would say that. I must, I suppose. Still, we shall be leaving here in a few days. And she is not likely ever to see him again. Would it not be best —" She left the thought unfinished.

"No, it would not. She'll be doing nothing but thinking of him, you know." He spoke with authority. The voice of experience.

"You are right, of course." They were strolling

slowly now, to the annoyance of those behind them. "It is just that I hate to — Only" — she brightened — "it should not be as bad as it might have been. At least she is in transports at the moment." She went on to tell Rupert of her aunt's literary accomplishment.

He was properly impressed. "Well, I'm flabbergasted!" They walked on while he appeared to be digesting this turn of events. "Are you glad or sorry?" he asked abruptly.

"Why, what an odd question. I am glad of course."

"You are?" He sounded crestfallen.

She looked indignant. "Why on earth should I be sorry for my aunt's success? What do you take me for?"

"Oh." His face cleared. "You thought I was talking about the book. What I mean to say is, are you sorry to be leaving London?"

She hesitated. "N-no. I shall not be sorry to leave — London."

"You don't sound quite sure," he prodded.

"Well, you surely can't expect me to say I shall be sorry to leave you, after all that has passed between us."

His voice was husky. He could not look at her. "Expect, no. Hope, yes."

Evelina stopped all traffic once again. Her eyes were shining. "Oh, Rupert." She tugged at his sleeve and forced him to look at her directly. "You aren't saying that you still retain some feelings for me, are you?"

"No, I ain't saying it. For this is hardly the time and place."

"Well, it is the only time and place we are likely to have," she pointed out practically.

"All right, then, damn it all, I am still in love with you. Thought I could get over it, but there it is."

"Oh, thank God."

"Really? Thank God? Oh, I say! Is it possible? Does that mean?"

"Of course it does. Only how embarrassing. What do we do now?"

"Well, we won't go to Gretna Green, that is for sure." He took her arm, and they moved on with the crowd.

"No indeed." She shuddered. "I hate the very sound of that place." She was thinking hard. "I collect that I should tell you that Lady Harville has invited me to come back here next Season and make my come-out."

"Oh?" His face was expressionless. "And is that what you wish?"

"Not really. It seems rather pointless."

"I agree. I don't want you on the Marriage Mart."

"I had much rather just make my bow at Fairwood. If only —"

"That would be famous! For I plan to talk Thornton into letting me have another go at managing the Yorkshire estate. And if I do well, it would not amaze me at all if he gave it to us for a wedding present."

"Now, *that* would be famous!" There were stars in Evelina's eyes as she looked up at Rupert adoringly.

The temptation was much too powerful to resist. He guided her into relative privacy behind a booth and kissed her. An activity that rapidly became habit-forming till finally she rallied sufficiently to push herself away.

"Oh, my heavens. I told Aunt Claudia that I would only be gone a moment. We must be getting back."

He responded, reluctantly, to her sense of urgency. But as they hurried back again along the path, he did say rather anxiously, "This does mean that we are re-betrothed, you realize."

"Of course. I have never really felt unbetrothed, actually, when it comes down to it. But aunt is still going to ring a peal over me."

Claudia did no such thing, however. For when the breathless pair reached the iron bench, she was gone. "Went off with a soldier, she did," the fat lady, still munching apples, informed them.

Chapter Twenty-four

Claudia had been so lost in thought that Hugo seemed a figment of her imagination. "What are you doing here?" she blurted when reality set in.

"I had to see you."

"Did you not get my letter? And how on earth did you find me in this mob?"

"I followed you. Claudia, we must talk."

The fat lady had been looking with increasing interest from the smartly dressed young lady in the pale green walking dress and bonnet to the handsome officer in his scarlet coat. Claudia had been about to tell Hugo that they had nothing whatsoever to say to one another, that the time for such a conversation had long since passed them by, but she was reluctant to continue entertaining this stranger. "Very well, then." She gave in with a decided lack of enthusiasm. "But only for a moment. Evelina should be back soon."

Hugo led her swiftly toward the Serpentine and an arrangement of shrubbery that offered a limited bit of privacy. "Oh, do get on with it," Claudia thought irritably as she hurried along with him. "We do not need seclusion."

She glanced at the handsome profile and was amazed at how little it now moved her. Did it, in fact, look weak? Effeminate, perhaps? What was it one heard about scales falling from the eyes?

Could that have happened to her unawares? For now it was difficult to understand the heart-burnings of so many years. Perhaps her tastes had simply changed.

The major reached his spot. It was not entirely private. There was no such thing in Hyde Park on this particular day. But he led her through the screening foliage to the water's edge, out of earshot, at least, of the passersby, where they could appear to be admiring the model warships in formation awaiting the fake battle. He glanced furtively all around to establish that they were unobserved, then grasped her hands and gazed tenderly into her eyes. "I love you, Claudia," he said huskily.

"Fustian."

"But it is true." His voice was ardent. "You are the only woman I have ever loved."

"Indeed? Then, may I say you chose a very odd way of showing it."

"Oh, I cannot blame you for being bitter. I can imagine your hurt and humiliation. But try to understand. I was young and homesick. We were apart. And would be for aeons, so it seemed. So when Maria threw herself at me — well, you know what soldiers are — I was too weak to resist. And after that one unforgivable mistake, there was no choice left me. I had to marry her."

"Are you trying to tell me, Hugo, that you were seduced?" She was hard put not to laugh.

"I am trying to tell you," he replied with a dignity that made her a bit ashamed of her near levity, "that while what I did is indefensible, the truth remains that you are the only woman I have loved. And what is more, I know that you love me, too. You cannot deny it."

"Oh, but I do deny it. For it simply is not so."

Once more Claudia realized that she was telling the absolute, liberating truth. When had the change happened? she wondered. While crossing Grosvenor Square perhaps?

"I won't believe that. Your constancy betrays you. You have been true to me all these years, Claudia. If you do not still love me, why have you not married?"

She longed to tell him how weary she was of being asked that very question and that her answer never satisfied anyone, especially herself. Instead she took another stab at explanation. "I collect it is because eligible suitors are not exactly thick on the ground in our vicinity, as you should remember." She managed to extract her hands.

"Humbug. That is only an excuse. A woman as lovely as you could never want for suitors. You do love me. I know you do. And now that fate has brought us together again, I will not allow us to be parted."

"Oh, indeed? Are you not forgetting a little matter of a wife and child. Or is it children?"

"I have it all worked out." He tried, unsuccessfully, to clasp her hands again. "I will arrange to be posted here in London and buy a house for you. We can be together, then, the way we were meant to be. And in the sight of God, you will be my one true wife."

"Hugo!" She was not believing what she had just heard. "Are you offering me a carte blanche?"

"I am offering you my heart, which you have always had," he said. And oblivious to whoever might be watching and before she could react, he took her in his arms and was bending his head to kiss her when a heavy hand clapped down upon his shoulder.

"I would suggest that you release my wife," Lord Thornton said.

Major Landseer did just that, spinning conveniently around so that his lordship was able to land a punishing left hook to his jaw. The blow was sufficiently staggering to make it an easy task for the peer to shove the major into the Serpentine.

"Come along, now," Thornton smiled at Claudia. "They're all waiting for us."

"But shouldn't we pull Hugo out? He could very well drown."

"Not a chance. All that perfection could be mud-covered, however. Which, I confess, I should like to see. But as I said, we have kept the others waiting long enough."

He offered her his arm with a slight bow, much as if he planned to take her in to dinner. She placed her hand upon it, slightly dazed.

"There was no need for all that, you know. I would have extricated myself."

"I know." He laughed suddenly. "But it felt damned good."

They threaded their way through the crowd without speaking for a bit. Claudia was trying, unsuccessfully, to make sense of the previous scene. There was definitely a need for clarification.

"There is one thing I do not understand. Why did you say what you did?"

"What did I say when, love?" He looked puzzled.

"Just before you hit him. You said, 'Let go of my wife.'"

"Did I?" He frowned in concentration. "I do believe you are right. But dashed if I exactly remember the why of it. Could be I thought the words would have a familiar ring. I don't doubt he's heard the phrase enough times for it to strike terror into his heart. But no," he mused aloud, "that can't be it. I must have been considering your sensibilities."

"My sensibilities? 'Let go of my wife'? How was that supposed to help my sensibilities?"

He pulled her off the path for a moment to allow four lads with hoops the right-of-way.

"Well, I did consider, 'Let go of my fiancée.'" He resumed the conversation as they walked on. "But I rejected the notion. Didn't think you'd care for it."

"But wife would be perfectly acceptable?" She stared up at him in disbelief.

"I certainly thought so. Pardon me if I am

wrong, of course, but I collect you must have had your fill of being a fiancée. You were one for donkey's years, were you not? The memory could not be pleasant. So I thought we would omit that part and go straight to the nuptials."

"You thought what?"

She came to a sudden halt. He tugged her along.

"My dear Claudia," he said patiently, "your ears are perfectly sound. I do wish I could say as much for your understanding."

"There is nothing wrong with that, either, for I know you are not making me an offer. I distinctly remember your words to my brother: 'Me, marry Miss Wentworth?'" she mimicked. "'The notion is absurd.'"

"Oh, God," he groaned. "I had hoped you had forgot that."

"Hardly." She suddenly laughed. "Even Hugo was less insulting. He just now offered me a carte blanche." The notion struck her as irresistibly funny.

He waited patiently till she wiped the tears away. "A carte blanche, eh? Of course, if that is what you prefer — But I was thinking more along the lines of parson's mousetrap."

"You are offering for me!"

"Well-done! Good girl! At last you've noticed."

"But that is absurd."

"Please, not again. We've been through all that. And I happen to think we will deal famously. I say, could we get out of this crowd?"

Though he did not realize it, Lord Thornton guided Miss Wentworth behind the same booth that his brother had utilized so effectively a little earlier. But being older and considerably more practiced, he was able to top his sibling's performance by quite a margin. "I do love you, you know," he declared huskily at the kiss's conclusion.

She was still clinging to him, her face pressed against his shoulder. There was barely enough breathing room to murmur, "And I you. By the by, who is Sophy?"

He pushed her back an arm's length, in order to direct a censorious look on target. "That, Miss Wentworth, is a very inappropriate question that I shall pretend I did not hear. Do you wish to rob our marriage of all mystery? Come on. Our group will be forming a search party soon."

"You are right, of course." She sounded chastened. "It is not necessary to know everything about one's intended." As they walked along, she mulled over what she had just said and came to a resolution. "However, I do fear there is something about me you really should know."

"Lord help us. Surely there's not another Hugo in your closet."

"No, nothing like that."

"What a relief. Then you are referring to your literary life, perhaps? By the by, congratulations on your recent success."

She was stopped in her tracks once more. "How did you know about that?"

He tugged her on. "My aunt told me. She is bursting with pride you know. But I'm puzzled. Why such a need to confess? Your writing should present no problem. That is," he was struck by a sudden thought, "not unless you'd expect me to read your stuff. You wouldn't, would you?" he asked anxiously.

She choked, but managed to shake her head.

"Well, that's all right, then.

"As I was saying, you can have a whole wing of the house for your efforts and write to your heart's content. Between lyings-in, of course." He grinned salaciously when she blushed.

"Oh, thank goodness, you found her!" Evelina exclaimed in relief as they approached the large tent set up for tea. Their party, with the addition — to no one's surprise — of Rupert Hunt, was seated around a table sharing an aromatic pot and a heaping plate of assorted cakes. "We were so worried when we learned you had gone off with that dreadful man!" A mouthful of seedcake blurred her words a bit, but there was no mistaking their solemnity. "Thank heavens, Lord Thornton said he would see to it. This is not the proper time to tell you what Rupert and I have just found out about your long-lost major. But be warned. You must have nothing more to do with him."

"Let me assure you that she will not." Thornton pulled Claudia closer to him in a decidedly possessive manner. "Sir Galahad has slain her dragon, and Miss Wentworth has promised to be his — that is to say my wife."

Congratulations were immediate and sincere, albeit the majority of the party could not help but appear astonished. Lady Harville, however, looked smug.

Mr. Stanesby appeared bemused. He was staring back and forth from Claudia to Thornton with beetled brow, obviously in the unfamiliar throes of thought. Then, of a sudden, the light dawned. "I knew it!" he crowed. "Dashed, if I didn't always know that I had seen you before, Miss Wentworth. And now that you and Thorn stand there together, it all comes back. It was that night at Hunter's Hall when you interrupted the card game and —" He stopped mid-sentence, appalled at what he had just said. His face flamed red.

"Well, that's dished us," Thornton grinned at Claudia. "We haven't a moment to lose before your reputation's shredded. It's off to Gretna Green for us."

"Do not even consider such a thing." Lady Harville frowned her disapproval. "You will be married properly from Fairwood, unless, of course, Sir Edwin objects, which seems unlikely. But if so, Harville House and St. Paul's will do nicely. It certainly behooves you to set a proper example for these youngsters." She smiled indulgently at Evelina and Rupert, who looked sheepish. "Indeed, I insist upon it."

Just then a series of earsplitting explosions, like the sounds of artillery firing rapidly, sent their party scurrying from the tea tent. "Fireworks, by George!" Rupert shouted.

Rockets were being launched toward the darkening sky from every possible tree and lamppost. They went off singly and in clusters, spreading above the gaping crowd like young stars in the making. Time was suspended until the last burst had faded.

"Well, now, that truly concludes it," Mr. Stanesby remarked philosophically as the last star burst faded. "London has celebrated the war's end in high style and to exhaustion. Those fireworks were the last hurrah. Now it is all over."

"Oh, I would not say so," Lord Thornton observed. "It is all in the point of view, old fellow. I would say that those fireworks foretell a new and glorious beginning."